Princess And Gore

Princess And Gore

Jim Christy

Canadian Cataloguing in Publication Data

Christy, Jim
Princess and Gore.

Novel
ISBN 1-896860-86-9

I. Title.
Ps8555.H74P74C38 2000 C813'.54 C00-910927-7
PR9199.3.C4982P74 2000

Cover Art: Maurice Spira

Published in 2000 by:
Ekstasis Editions Canada Ltd.
Box 8474, Main Postal Outlet
Victoria, B.C. V8W 3S1

Ekstasis Editions
Box 571
Banff, Alberta TOL OCO

Princess and Gore has been published with the assistance of a grant from the Canada Council and the Cultural Services Branch of British Columbia.

Sure, Princess and Gore Streets don't intersect but they used to; the original Princess Street being what is now known, east of Main, as Pender Street.

Britt Hagarty, 1949-1999, writer and musician, knew this kind of thing, and most everything else about the street, and a lot more besides, and it is to his memory that *Princess and Gore* is dedicated.

CHAPTER ONE

Gene Castle woke with the first note of the ship's whistle. It was as if the guy in the engine room pulled on the whistle chain and yanked him from the land of dreams. In a panic that he'd be too late to make the ship, Castle was about to leap out of bed and grab his seabag for if he missed the ship, the agents of the communists or the agents of the fascists, one or the other, would nab him there in Marseilles for sure.

But there was something familiar about the wallpaper, that grandad's scarf of a pattern, and the rug too with nappy faded roses, the scarred nightstand and noisy metal Russian alarm clock, its clapper and two bells like onion domes on a St. Petersburg cathedral—make that the Leningrad Central Party Headquarters; and he didn't have his clothes on either which, more than anything else, told him he wasn't in a cheap hotel room in Marseilles' old port, ready to hit the floor running. Castle realized—and from opening his eyes to realizing only took about five seconds—that he was in a cheap hotel room in the old port section of Vancouver, and that there had been a ship's whistle but it was probably nothing more than a CP Liner at the foot of Shanghai Alley ready to take some swells over the swells on a slow cruise to China or maybe down Mexico way. There'd be shuffleboard and quoits, and a ship's band doing their utmost every night to duplicate the very best of Paul Whiteman, and that certainly wasn't going to make any waves.

All that made him happy, and the warmth of the body at his back made him even happier. Louise Jones, sound asleep next to him in the Rose Hotel like so many other mornings over the years. He knew that in a few minutes the Russian alarm clock would go off like the Kronstadt Mutiny and he'd have to hammer it into submission; Louise would murmur and move right into him, and they might make a few sounds of their own.

Three mornings back in town after three years gone. They'd reached Spain a couple of weeks after the revolt of the Morocco generals, tramped over the mountains, making Barcelona just as the Durutti column was rushing to Saragossa. Buenaventura Durutti that grand fanatic. The CNT renounces everything but victory in the war; Durutti had said it so many times. That bank robber, that anarchist, that hero. Castle had been about ten steps from the man, just outside the Clinical Hospital, when the bullets mowed him down in Mardrid that first November. That was at the very beginning of the long tragedy. The fascists and the Nazis were having their little warm up, Spring Training, and the bleachers were full of nations with the scorecards hiding their eyes. And now the season had started with a successful road trip through Poland.

Rrrraaarrnnnggg! went the alarm clock, and Castle pounded it with the heel of his hand. Politeness wouldn't work, neither would manly firmness, you had to bludgeon the thing into submission, it being loud enough to wake major league rubbies from a sterno sleep.

Louise Jones murmured and murmured again and wriggled in the warmth of the sheets. She moved a few inches until she was full up against Castle, nudged him with a knee, then turned from her right side onto her left side. Castle responded to the invitation by turning on his left side, putting his right arm over her right shoulder as she pressed her rear end against him.

Eleven minutes later, they were sitting up in bed, backs against the headboard, Louise had the sheet up just above her nipples and was looking down at her chest. "Another exciting morning in Vancouver," she said.

"Watching your blush disappear."

"When it stops appearing is when we're in trouble."

"Must be something in the literature about that," Castle said. "The medical literature."

"Or in that book, who's is it—Krafft-Ebbing?"

"Yeah, the chapter on ebbing and flowing of passion."

"If I knew how to mimic it, I could teach it to bored housewives save them all that fake moaning and screaming."

"That's not what bored housewives need."

"Speaking of fake moaning and screaming. That tattooed carney bitch you were frittering away your time with when I first became aware of you with Baker Shows. What was her name?"

"Not this again. Why am I telling myself you know damn well what her name was?"

"I assure you that I do not. Oh, wait, it just came to me: Lydia."

"Just like that."

"That dame was louder than your goddamned Commie alarm clock. And me just an innocent from Hardisty."

"Let's keep this in perspective, Louise. You were, afterall, a kooch girl in a carnival. As for her noise making, she wasn't faking it either."

"You men. What do you know?"

"Louise, tell me something, you ever give much thought to the different kinds of reactions? I mean how some women really get with some banshee wailing..."

"Your five-alarm frails."

"Yeah, but most just make some pleasant groaning noises. Others are silent."

"Maybe they're asleep."

"There's that too."

"What's really awful, downright offensive," said Louise. "Is men who make a lot of noise. Like wart hogs with a heart condition. Like donkey engines."

"You've had a lot of experience with men of that sort?"

"A couple, I must admit, but before your time, of course."

"Of course, remarkable indeed since I haven't seen you for nearly a year."

"Nor me you. What were you doing?"

"Dodging bullets, sneaking over international borders."

"That kind of activity can inflame the passions. Ah, hell, Gene enough of that kind of crap. I missed you, baby. There was nobody else."

"We're a pair Louise, even when we're apart."

"Yeah, but Lydia. Whatever happened to her? That bitch was so old most of her tattooes had faded. Probably wound up pedalling her ass at migrant labour camps."

"I heard she married a publican in the east end of Toronto and had lots of babies."

"Yeah, and I bet they all came out illustrated."

"Forget blushing. That would be a real gaff."

"Wish you could make me scream like that."

"Well I could try."

Louise Jones came out of the washroom all dressed and made up, struck a pose. "Think I'll get the part?"

"Yeah, if you're auditioning for a blue movie."

"Wars are great for hemlines."

"If one has the legs for it, which you do."

"Give him a little bit twice and he still flatters, what a guy."

"I know, I'm a prince and a paragon," Castle said, grabbing the double-breasted jacket of his dark blue suit from the back of the room's only chair and donning his brand-new charcoal grey fedora. "And soon to be a pauper if I don't get something happening."

"Yeah, me too. I only have half an hour before showtime. Got to put these legs to use while I still have them. It's hell when a woman passes forty, Gene."

"Past forty!" Castle exclaimed, reaching for the door. "But you told me...."

Cordova Street, eight-thirty in the morning, was on the hustle. It was on the hustle every morning but Castle had never seen it anything like this. Sidewalks jammed, trucks, cars, horns and shouts. It was a hop-head of a day adawning. There seemed to be a jump beat to the thing. Some wild band laying down rhythm for the street jive. A few weeks into a brand new war and all atwitter. Mid-October, Indian summer threw fairy dust over everything, a faintly golden benzedrine patina.

They were unloading trucks double-time. North Van shipyards

working triple shifts. Clang clang say the streetcars, cling cling the cash registers. So long Depression. Front page of the Times had photos of kids and grownups all with their faces aglow and the cutline: "Off to the War with a Smile." Yes, indeedy everybody seemed to be smiling, men—boys, really—marching away with the cocky insouciance of being eighteen and immortal, going to clout that kraut but not too quickly, knock him around but not out, not for a few months, not until those contracts are filled and the country's on its feet again.

"Say, what's going on at Manny's?" Castle thrust his chin in the direction of a shop near the corner of Main.

"He's having the place redone. Carpenters and painters in there for a couple of weeks."

"Hey, Manny!"

"Hello, Gene. Louise, you get better looking every day."

"What's happening?" Castle said to the fat grinning bald man.

"Nobody wants Good Junk anymore. They got money for New Stuff. How do you like that for a name, eh? Manny's New Stuff?"

"Real swell, Manny. You're gonna be rolling in dough."

"Yes sir. Everybody's going to make some moo-la now, even the main meshugginer, my brother-in-law."

Without changing his jovial expression or the timbre of his voice, Manny added, "So Gene I've heard stories about your adventures. Stop by, maybe we should talk."

They gave Manny a wave, and reached the corner with the photographer's shop. Gene had always liked the window of the place because it seemed to offer its own little glimpse into the community. Whenever he got back into town, no matter after how long a time, Castle went to the photographer's window to see what had changed. And it seemed an accurate replica of the neighborhood, what with retouched photos from the old country, grandma and grandpa on the day they left the village, pictures of new immigrants from the four corners of the earth, newly marrieds and babies on the rug. Now most of these were pushed to the perimeter, and at the centre of the window were eight-by-tens of young men, and some older ones, in uniform. As many years as he'd been passing the place, Castle had gotten only rare glimpses of the photographer himself, a tall and gangly man with deep set eyes, lank hair that hung down and which he probably had to push back a thousand times a day. Castle imagined his hair coated with fixative.

"Business is looking up," Louise said.

"Yeah, you got to have a picture of your son, your grandson, your husband in their nice new uniform. Put it on the mantel or on top of the radio."

"You can look at the picture smiling back at you while the announcer reads the latest news from the battlefields."

Gene and Louise kept walking. They were business people just like everyone else on the street. Even that strange panhandler across the way out front of the brand new store selling sporting goods. What's the guy doing in monk's robes? Maybe he's a monk. He's talking a mile a minute but there was no time to go over and catch his spiel. Louise had an audition and he had a breakfast to eat and a brand new office to go to. Actually it was the old office except he hadn't been there for three years. He pictured somebody with cobwebs in the anteroom. Sorry to have kept you waiting, madam. Hope it's not important.

No, he'd cleared out of the office before clearing out of the country, bound for Spain with Louise and Frontenac, the reporter. just after that trouble with the Italians. Castle heard that the office was taken over by a fellow who sat hunkered over a table all day with a light and a magnifying glass getting diamonds to look all glittery. The fellow had made a lot of money and had to move to bigger quarters on account of all the people he had to hire. So Castle couldn't claim the office was jinxed. Not that he'd ever used that excuse but he'd had it ready just in case.

They reached Hastings and Main, and Louise's bus stop, when their attention was drawn to a commotion on the other side of the street. A group of people at the opening to Hogan's Alley seemed to be looking at something on the ground. Crossing Hastings to the southeast corner, Castle and Louise noticed that several of the people in the knot were Negroes, not a common sight or even an uncommon sight anywhere in Vancouver except right around here, Hogan's Alley, or up ahead on Union Street, at the Chicken Inn on Keefer, and maybe even a few blocks west on Homer. There were white people in this crowd, of course, and Chinese, a couple of Indians from India, and a couple of the native variety. This gaullifmaufry of the species was united by that most universal of characteristics: curiosity. They were curious about the man on the ground, a recently dead individual who'd soon be as stiff as the creases in the slacks of his tan garbadine suit. Castle noted his brown and white kicks, the way the toes pointed to the sides. The dead man had on a mostly snow-white shirt, with a diamond stick pin lifting the knot of a chocolate brown tie the same colour as his face. The man's otherwise immaculate ensemble was ruined by the blood that seeped from under and around the second button of his tan garbadine jacket. There was an aureloe of blood around his head. But a dead Negro man in a spreading pool of blood was not even what really held everyone's attention. No, they were staring at a yellow shoe, the high heel of which was imbedded in the man's head.

"Would you look at that," Louise muttered.

"What're you two gawking at? Never seen a high heel sticking in a shine's head before?"

They looked toward the voice. It came out of a police detective who hadn't taken any fashion tips from the dapper deceased. Not one of Detective Koronicki's suits had ever been in a laundry unless it was on his person when he rousted stowaways from the pressing machines. He could have hung his ties in a modern art gallery. After he got promoted off the beat, Koronicki's colleagues had given him a hairbrush for a Christmas present. Scuttlebutt had it that the hair brush remained undisturbed in Koronicki's desk for twenty years or until he no longer had even fluff to ruffle, at least not enough to warrant the fiction that he'd get around to using it some day.

"Plenty of times," Castle said, "Detective Koronicki. In plenty of places."

"Yeah, I know all about your career chock full of incident. So then what seems to have you mum with wonder?"

"It's you, Detective. I not only wonder that you haven't retired yet. I wonder that you're still standing."

"Louise, don't let this fellow get on the wrong side of me or it's him that won't be standing."

The Detective tipped Castle the wink and started to move off. "Come over here you two. Gene, I mean, Castle, I want to ask you a few questions."

"Just a minute," Louise said. "I'd love to stay for the badinage between..."

"The what?" said Koronicki.

"You two guys trying to be witty with each other, pretending to dislike each other or like each other whichever it is you're going to pretend to do, but I got an audition to make. So excuse me if I make an exit."

"Nice to see you again, Louise."

"Likewise Detective. That's a cute trick. The high heel to the head. I'll remember that."

Louise walked off, Castle glancing over his shoulder for a glimpse of seamed stocking below the fluttering hem of her skirt.

He moved to the edge of the gaggle of cops and gawkers and waited while the Detective gave instructions. When Koronicki joined him again, Castle was surprised by the Detective's grin and awkward pat on the shoulder.

"Never had the chance to stand you a drink or anything like that," the rumpled cop rumbled. "That Garmano collar back in '36 earned me a nice little raise."

"Well then it's more than a drink you owe me. But it's been three years so I can wait a little longer. Still I'm wondering what questions you got for me. As you can see I got on two black brogans and not one yellow high heel so it couldn't have been me done this foul deed."

"I don't got no questions for you but I have to act stern because..."

"Because you are stern. Today's ebullience is the exception that proves the you-know-what."

"Listen Weismuller...."

"You mean Weisenheimer? Or do you think we're getting along swimmingly? Or even swingingly?"

"Huh?"

"Never mind."

"Yeah, well, listen, you know I can't fraternize with you in public on account of you're probably getting back in the same line of work, and we may wind up in positions potentially fraught with conflict so we got to at least appear vaguely hostile."

"I like that: 'positions potentially fraught with conflict.' What you mean is, I'll be in the chair under the bare light bulb for six or seven hours while that bog-trotting partner of yours works out."

"Don't have no bog-trotting partner no more. Got a grim Glaswegian which is him over there now, the pint-sized party with the notebook. He, or is it him, about whom you speak was stupid enough to try to put the arm on Skinny O'Day's working girls. Now he's a nighwatchman in London, Ontario."

"About his speed, nothing to watch."

"Good riddance to em. But Gene, you're right it's more than a drink I'm into you for. Never know when you might need a chum on the force."

Castle nodded. "Now I got a question for you. How come you didn't retire, nice little raise not withstanding?"

"Ah, what would I do? And anyway crime's on the rise. Before, you had your gangsters and grifters, sure, but mostly what went on was gas station heists, drugstore robberies, guy on the corner selling apples got knocked over, desperate capers by desperate men what maybe hadn't had a bite to eat in three days. But the Depression's over and some folks is feeling frisky."

"The deceased on the ground over there, was he feeling frisky?"

Koronicki glanced at his own notebook. "Moncrieff Dilman, age 29, out of Halifax, Nova Scotia. You know, Africville. Suspect in custody name of Darlene Steadman, also of Halifax. She took off her yellow spike and hit Moncrieff upside the head after determining he was paying undue attention to one Lorraine Hightower, a fancy number just hit our quaint burg from the bright lights of East Oakland, California. She has also been taken away and is supposed to be booked for, if you'll pardon the expression, disturbing the piece. Lorraine slugged Darlene when Darlene shoe-ed —I suppose you might call it— Moncrieff. And this, in turn, so angered Darlene that she stabbed poor Moncrieff who was, according to the accounts of eyewitnesses, staggering around the Scat Cat Club with a stunned expression wondering what in hell had happened and why his head felt so funny. People in the club, a few of whom were Caucasian, were heard to admit that it *was* rather funny. At least until

Darlene buried the blade. A mean woman, that's a fact."

"How'd Moncrieff get all the way out to the street?"

"You're thinking like a genuine private eye. Moncrieff was one tough dude. Shoe-ed and shanked, he staggered out into Hogan's, possibly, given his confused state, hoping to call at another afterhours joint. Then he changed his mind and sought a comfortable place on the asphalt. Had a thick roll of twenties in his pocket so like the song says, he died standing pat."

"Or like the other song says, he died lying in a pool of blood with a blade in his belly and a yellow shoe in his head."

"Yeah. So, you see, Castle, this is not your Depression-era sort of crime. We done turned that corner Prosperity was just around. Why, lad, there were not three nightclubs and four afterhours joints in one itsy bitsy alley a few months ago. We didn't have Negroes killing each other while jungle music was playing at eight-thirty of a Thursday morning. So could you picture me on the police pension playing solitaire at the kitchen table out in Marpole while all this was going on?"

"I guess not, Detective Koronicki. You're a credit to your race."

"Thanks, Castle. See you around."

Chapter Two

The big window of the place on the corner of Carrall and Pender Streets was so steamed up, the uninitiated would never know there was a Ramona's Deluxe Cafe half an inch away. The window had been steamed up since Castle was a kid and he'd meet his old man there when the old man came into town off a job in the bush somewhere. They had probably been steamed up in the late-Eighties when Ramona, whoever she was, opened the place. In the late-Eighties Vancouver consisted of a sawmill by the salt chuck and a saloon owned by a blowhard called Gassy Jack Deighton, and Matty Muldoon down the counter with his thick fingers around a thick cup of tea had known Gassy Jack personally. Hell, Matty Muldoon was the only person still extant who knew who Ramona was, a subject on which he had never pronounced. Anyway, the owner, Mr. Tommy Chew had been at the grill when Castle was a little boy, and he was at the grill now, his spatula like a conductor's baton. If you inquired after his sons or his wife, or commented on the weather, Mr. Tommy Chew answered you in Manadarin, or sometimes he started a conversation with you in Mandarin but he spoke perfect grill-man's English, "Order Up!... Got two on a raft with oars...Want em blinded, shining, what?...What, eh?"

Matty Muldoon had a face like a sun-scorched walnut and eyelids so wrinkled you could barely make out two slits of blue. He smiled yellow stumps of teeth at Castle and touched the brim of a seaman's cap. Castle nodded back, he'd known the man forever; his father had known him, maybe his grandfather. He was a walking talking history of seafaring but Castle doubted the rumour Matty used to pal with Captain Vancouver.

Maude set down a black coffee and didn't need to ask him what he wanted even though it had been three years since he last ordered. Not much ever changed in Ramona's. It was a refuge from the street. Once you passed some never defined test which was strictly intuitive but consisted of hanging around for awhile without doing anything to upset the harmony of the place, well, then, you could use Ramona's as an office, for a tryst, or hide from the law amongst the spuds in the cellar.

There at the counter, a couple of stools down from Matty Muldoon, were Guy Roberts the king of sugar and Raymond Thomas, who passed as his chauffeur. Given what Castle had just witnessed at Hogan Alley's, he realized Raymond Thomas's place as the only Negro around had been usurped. Thomas came from Saltspring, one of the Gulf Islands just off the mainland. His ancestors settled there in the middle of the nineteenth century, having chartered a boat from San Francisco fleeing the racial situation in the land of the free. Guy Roberts had worked on fishing boats that called at Saltspring and the two men became friends. Roberts was full of ambition but his dreams were thwarted because he was also illiterate; Raymond Thomas was a brilliant young man, highly literate, but his dreams were thwarted because he was not a Caucasian. Thomas taught Roberts to read and write, and guided his career. From the day the two met, they'd been at each other's side; Thomas first posing as errand boy, later as a chauffeur. But mostly he was strategist and financial adviser. In Ramona's, they could drop the act. But every so often, the stress of not seeing any of his own kind, had sent Raymond off on a three-day bender which came to be known euphemistically as "looking for another Negro." Like: "What the hell happened to you, Raymond? Where you been?"

"Sorry, Guy. I went looking for another negro."

"You find one?"

"Yeah, and this other negro? He says it might be wise to invest in plastics."

And they were each worth a million and counting.

"Hey, Gene old buddy."

The man in the jacket and tie was his own age, early forties, and slender with a narrow, weathered face. He held out a hand. "Long time, pal."

Castle took the hand, shook it, stared into the guy's eyes for a second before muttering, "Jesus."

"Naw, it's just you're old partner, Frank."

"Frank Evans, as I live and breath."

"Well you don't have to look so astonished. Just because I got on a monkey suit and I combed my hair this morning."

"That's exactly why I am so astonished. I've never seen you with a jacket and tie or with your hair combed either, as a matter of fact."

"Hell, Gene, you've also probably never seen me when when I wasn't at least half in the bag. That last time? You know, when you and Louise and that Frontenac were getting on the ship, the bottom of Shanghai Alley. Me and old Johnny and Rose went with you in the cab? I was three sheets to the wind then."

"You always held it well."

"Yeah, on the outside. I've been sober for four months."

"Good for you, Frank. You're not going to preach to me are you?"

"Hell, no. Ruin a friendship? I said, I'm on the wagon not off my rocker. I got a job too. Two jobs actually. Picture me—a salesman?"

"I guess I'll have to start."

"Yeah, I got two lines. One of them's encyclopedias. The Britannica, eh? I remember right you had half an old set."

"Not just any old set, it was the Coronation Edition."

Castle had taken half a set from a client as a retainer and in lieu of standard payment. It was a Shaughnessy Heights dame who hired him to discover the identity of the woman under whose bed her hubbie was putting his shoes. Castle did the job but the client had an unfortunate accident before he could collect the other half of the set. It seemed she herself was keeping outside company, and with Manny Chung, the gambler, of all people. It was a boating accident. Manny drowned and the dame got her throat slashed by the propeller blade.

"And I only got volumes fourteen and up. I just started volume fifteen, 'Maryb to Mushe,' and I'm going to read about Mascara which not only is something women put on their eyelids but is mainly a town in Algeria with good white wines. I went from Masaryk to Mascara, having skipped Masaya."

"Why the hell did you do that?"

"What?"

"Skip Whaddayacallit?"

"Masaya. It's in Nicaragua and that's where I was back in '25 when the U.S. Marines invaded. Of course, they were always invading. Hid out for four days in the shack of an Indian coffee plantation foreman and revolutionary sympathizer."

"So you want the first half maybe we can work something out."

"Has to be the Coronation Edition."

"That sold out immediately."

"Uh huh. You know, it must be right what everybody says."

"About what?"

"The new boom in the economy. I mean, if an old anarcho-syndicalist reprobate like you has got not one but two jobs, and in sales, no less, there certainly is a whole new attitude and we've turned the corner for sure."

"Yeah, I guess so. Hey, Gene. You don't want any new encyclopedias, how bout a vacuum cleaner? Keep that office of yours looking good, put the client at ease not seeing dust balls in the corners."

"Anybody desperate enough to come to me doesn't care about dustballs in the corners."

Castle, carrying two cardboard cups of coffee, kicked at the revolving door of the office building and crossed the imitation marble floored lobby to where Laura Easely sat at her switchboard.

"Hey, I see you're wearing mascara," he said, handing her one of the cups.

"Thanks. So? What's so surprising about that?"

"Nothing. Look..."

"I'd love you to stay and flirt with me, Gene. But duty bids me to tell you you got a client."

"A client? I'm not even officially open for business yet. In fact, I'm not even all that sure, I want to open for business."

"You spent all day yesterday carrying your furnishings—at least, you call them furnishings; I'd call them something else—up to the old room, you ought to go and face the music."

"Sure thing, kid. Is it a slinky dame with a husky seductive voice?"

"Maybe but if so she's hiding inside, way inside, the disguise of a fat guy about sixty, and there wasn't anything slinky about the way he took those stairs. Each step got both feet. Did have a husky voice though."

Castle looked toward the staircase and back at Laura who raised her eyebrows or rather the pencil line arcs where actual eyebrows used to be. He sighed and headed for the stairs.

The fat man was outside Gene Castle's office door studying his wristwatch when he heard the bannister creak. He looked up, watched Castle come walking toward him but didn't say anything until Castle was right there. "Okay, so you're not the bookmaker next door, eh? You must be the sometimes private investigator?"

The man reminded Castle of one those lead-bottomed toys—you could whack it as hard as you wanted to but you couldn't keep it down. He had thick glasses behind which hazel eyes seemed to float like marbles in aspic.

"That's right, I'm not the elusive Beanie Brown, just plain reliable Gene Castle."

"Reliable?" The man glanced at the frosted window of the office door upon which, in gilt letters, barely dry, was an announcement of sorts:

GENE CASTLE

9-?

—and glanced at his watch. Castle saw that the brown imitation-leather strap was frayed like flaking paint.

"So you're late. Your first day on the job."

"So sue me."

"So invite me in first."

The door opened onto what Castle, if he ever got the nerve, planned on referring to as his anteroom but which was actually two hard-backed chairs in front of two laquered Chinese-type screens.

Beyond the screens and across the room, with a backdrop of two tall, double-hung windows, was a six-foot long oak desk that yesterday had taken himself and three big former Wobblies to get up the stairs. Between the desk and the windows, on the other side of a sturdy swivel chair and on a shelf over the grey painted radiator, the half-set of the Coronation Edition stood at attention flanked by pairs of bricks. On top of each pair sat a bottle, one of rum, one of rye.

The other furnishings consisted of a driftwood hatrack, on which he hung his charcoal fedora, and another ladderback chair. There were framed photographs on the wall, one of a horse with a horseshoe of flowers over its neck; two of guys wearing nothing but shiny trunks and boxing gloves; a couple more of other fighters with rifles. In each of these, one of the guys was Gene Castle. There were also three masks, one from Dahomey, one done by Mosquito Indians of Honduras, and one by Haidas from up the coast.

"I notice you admiring my interior decoration," Castle said. "It's going to get even better soon's I add some items I've got in storage."

"Yeah" said the fat man. "If I was you, I'd have the client sign the contract on the other side of the screen before you bring them in here."

"Thanks for the advice, whoever you are."

"I'm Larry Sobell, your first client of the current season."

The man extended his hand and Castle took it. The palm was like a moist pad, the fingers so tapered that the tips were almost points.

"Please have a seat, Mr. Sobell, and tell me what I can do for you."

"What you can do for me is tell me who's sending me death threats. You want the job? How much will it cost me?"

"I don't know yet. This is your free consultation. How long have you been getting death threats?"

"Well they're not really death threats," the man said, reaching into the inside pocket of his pale grey and white seersucker suit.

"They're not?" Castle said. "Gee, I was just getting interested."

"Here, maybe you'll get more interested."

He handed over a dozen or so envelopes secured by a rubber

band, then folded his peculiar hands on a perfectly round belly that made Castle think Sobell had a globe of the world inside his clothes and his belt was the equator.

Castle saw that all the envelopes were addressed, by typewriter—the same typewriter—to L.I. Sobell. Inside, instead of death threats, were obituary notices. No accompanying message, nothing written in the margins. Just an obituary.

Castle looked again at the envelopes, at the postmarks.

"Each week for the last three months they've been coming," Sobell told him. "Every Friday."

"Anything else happen that might be connected? Phone calls?"

"No. Nothing I can think of."

"Anything out of the ordinary?"

"You mean, guys outside the house at night, other side of the street, lurking in the shadows watching my window?"

"Yeah, that sort of thing."

"No, nothing. Just these."

"You have enemies?"

"I've been in business for forty years, what'd you think? All those names of the people that died? They're all Jewish fellas, and I'm a Jewish fella. No kidding?—I hear you saying to yourself. Anyway, maybe it's some local minor league Nazi or something."

"Any of your Jewish friends get them?"

"My Jewish friends? I got other kinds? No, that's the thing, only me."

"What business are you in?"

The fat man shrugged his shoulders, a great big rising and falling of seersucker hills, "I do some of this, some of that. I started out with my father pushing a wheelbarrow in the schmatta trade, which means nothing to you."

"What do you think? I grew up in the forest? You think I'm some kind of kuni lemel?"

"So, I'm impressed, a goy who speaks like one of the tribe. You want the job, shamus—which is a word you probably think is Irish but is really Yiddish—you're hired."

"I want. I need."

"I pay. How much? You get a daily rate?"

"Not this job. A flat fifty and expenses."

The fat man rose from the chair, sighing as he straightened up, offered his paw again. "It's a deal. You're okay, I like you."

"I like you too but let's not the both of us get carried away."

"Funny fellow. I'll be on my way, keep me informed."

"Sure, just one thing, Mr. Sobell."

"Call me Larry."

"Larry. How'd you know it was my first day on the job?"

Sobell blinked, and removed his glasses. Castle wondered if it was a stall.

"The guy used to have this office..." Sobell took a grey handkerchief from his pocket and cleaned the lens, kept his eyes closed the whole time. "Young Nate Moscowitz. I know him since he was a baby, I knew his father. Every few weeks, I'd come visit, read to him while he polished his diamonds. So one time, he's not here. I ask the girl downstairs. She told me where he went and that some mysterious private eye was taking over who'd been here before. I think she's sweet on you, the girl."

Castle walked with Sobell to the other side of the Chinese screen, told him goodbye.

Sobell took hold of the door knob, said, "Eltsac eneG."

"What's that? 'See you around' in Yiddish?"

Sobell laughed, tapped the reinforced glass and walked out.

When the door closed, Castle looked at the glass, muttered, Yeah that's me all right, eltsaC eneG.

Castle took a sip of luke warm coffee and spread the envelopes out on the desk. Each envelope with its obituary notice on top. It appeared that all the obituaries, each of a Jewish man, were from the same newspaper. The paper and the typeface were uniform but they didn't put him in mind of the local rags, the Sun and the Times. Also, the biographical material stressed the activities of the deceased within the Jewish community in a way that implied the reader knew the who's, what's and where's. Take this poor unfortunate Mr. Levy; it said that Moise 'Moose' Levy prided himself on the fact that for twenty-three years consecutive years he served as such and such at the synagogue.

Now, the obit must be from a Jewish newspaper, Castle told himself, otherwise there would be an explanation of what such and such meant and, furthermore, if it was the Sun or the Times, the dimwit scribe would surely use the word, "Hebrew," as in "The local Hebrew community mourns the passing of...."

Speaking of dimwit local scribes, Castle mused, I have to go see old Joe—'I Was There'—Frontenac, who ought to be back in town now from his exciting adventures covering the new highway improvement project in the Fraser Valley. He considered Frontenac of the Times, and their capers of the past for at least a minute before beginning his examination of the postmarks on the envelopes. He liked the ones where the inked circle didn't completely mar the features of bland King George. Poor guy, he never wanted the job. But, alas, neither did his brother who up and abdicated. Poor shy George with his stutter, dreading those little speeches he has to make, pretending to be overjoyed to be paying a visit at all those outposts of the Empire where they have statues of some relative of his on horseback. Like our own little outpost where he was just a few weeks ago. Meanwhile, his drip of a brother gets to sit in the sun in Bermuda sipping Scotch and Soda, hoping for a little slap and tickle with that harridan he married. Please, oh pretty please, Wally. But, to be fair, Castle thought, and of course he was always fair, Wally is the real tragic figure in the play. All set to be the royal mistress, part of a fine tradition, and maybe even a power behind the throne, and Edward goes and pulls that stunt. Abdicating. Now the woman he loves has to look forward to a life of idleness without prestige while her husband grovels to the likes of Charles Bedaux and throws the salute to nasty little Adolph.

Snap out of it, already, Castle urged himself. Why worry about no-accounts like them? You got your own problems. Mainly you came back broke from three years of dangerous liason and undercover work in Spain. You're forty-three years old and back to scuffling for a living. Everybody else seems to have a job. They like the War. They don't know what they're in for.

Castle got out his Palm Dairy calender from the long centre desk drawer. It showed a picture of a couple of chubby five year olds with rosy cheeks and white outfits sitting on a porch swing with a glass of milk in their mitts. That's what we're fighting for! Of course, they could easily pass for German tykes.

Anyway, the dates on the postmarks—the ones that weren't smudged and unreadable—were all Thursdays, each a week apart. Sobell got an obit every Friday. Peering closely at the inked circle on one of the envelopes, thinking to himself, "I'm going to need reading glasses one of these years," Castle noted a little horizontal line, or rather, the suggestion of a line, where nine o'clock would be if the postmark were a clock. The little line was there on all the other postmarks too. He decided to nod knowingly the way a wise private eye ought to do. And after he'd done that very thing, Castle gathered up his obituaries and his envelopes, grabbed his fedora, and left his gorgeous office.

Laura was on the other side of her Dutch door, fingers plugging and unplugging wires. On the wall behind her were cubbyholes for mail and messages. On the desk to the right of her telephone board were two spikes where she impaled phone messages. A couple of times a day, she transferred messages from the spikes to the cubby holes. One spike was reserved for the bookie Beanie Brown's messages, the other spike for everyone else in the five-story office building.

Castle leaned on the half-door. Laura plugged a gap, saying, "No, he's not in. I'm not supposed to do this but, okay, go ahead."

She grabbed the pencil from behind her right ear. "Third Race. Peninsula Meadows. Townsend Toby, a double sawbuck across the board. Yeah, okay, Mr. Seattle Sims, I got it."

She unplugged the punter, looked at Castle, "Hell you want?"

"Only to lean here gazing on your graceful form, listening to the tremble of your vibrato."

"Cut the crap, Castle. You know damn well that for the last half-dozen years, you could have been grazing on my graceful form instead of gazing, and you could have done anything you pleased with my vibrato. I got damn sick of the ones that tried to make it tremble, and damn sick of making it tremble by my ownself. But you missed your chance, bub. I got a good man now. At least, I think he's a good man. Hope he is. We've only been out together twice."

"I wish you all the best, Laura. Or, maybe I should say: Again, I wish you all the best. And I have no hard feelings about the way you just put me in my place. I don't have any mail, eh?"

"No, you just got here from Spain."

"Well then let me take a look at somebody's else's mail."

"What're you talking about? You know it's against the law to open somebody's mail. I'll let you read some of the mash notes I get, if you want to."

"I don't want to read your mash notes or anyone else's. I just want to look at the envelopes."

"Like I always said, Gene. You're different from other men."

"I know that, doll. Just let me see a few. Hand me Beanie Brown's mail."

"Well, all right." Laurie snatched the mail from the bookie's cubby hole. "Why you doing this?"

Castle took them, looked close at the postmark on the top envelope, nodded. "It's just one of the tricks of the trade."

"Something you learned in that correspondance course for private operators you sent away for? The one advertised in the back of *Argosy* magazine?"

Castle stopped thumbing through the envelopes.

"Having a fella in your life sure makes you feisty."

He handed back the envelopes and thanked her.

"He's very, what'd'you call it—continental. Reminds me of that guy in the movies, Conrad something-or-other."

"Conrad Veidt?"

"Yeah, that's the one. Keeps me on my toes."

"Hey, don't tell me any embarrassing details."

"He's got a sexy scar on his cheek. Says he got it from duelling. Imagine that?"

"This continental gent wouldn't be from Germany, would he?"

"No, Switzerland."

"Yeah, that's what they all say."

"He makes me yodel too."

"I'd like to stay and hear more of your boasting but I'm on a case."

Chapter Three

Castle hit the street and crossed to the corner where the hump-backed Indian was selling newspapers.

"Hitler on the Move...Thousands of Canucks Enlist...Read all about it!...Hey, Gene Castle! Long time, no see. Glad you're still alive."

"Hey, Woody. So am I. Good to see you, old pal."

"Heard you bought it in Barcelona."

"No, I just rented it for a few days."

"Shouldn't joke about it, Gene. Better touch my hump for luck."

Castle touched Woody's hump, felt the weird hard cartilage under flannel.

"Thought you were going back to the reserve."

"I did, saw my ex-wife, realized why she's my ex-wife, and hightailed back here to the Big Smoke. You working?"

"Yeah. What I want to ask you: This typeface, this paper, mean anything to you? You know where it comes from?"

Castle showed a couple of the obits to the little man.

"It's not the *Sun* or the *Times* or that weekly they got out in Burnaby," Woody said. You want to find out, you go over to Granville, just the other side of Hastings. They got a new cigarstore-newstand over there. Carry all the papers, magazines. You want the Seattle paper, they got that."

"Who the hell'd want a Seattle paper?"

"Beats me, but some must."

"Okay, Gene.... Armstrong kayoes again.... Louis signs to fight Arturo Godoy.... Andy Hardy Gets Spring Fever.... Read all about it!"

Castle retraced his steps across Carrall Street and headed west. He glanced over at Shanghai Alley which was as bustling as ever, imagined it just as bustling underground as above ground. Still, the little street seemed somehow bereft of life now, like some of the spirit had gone out of it, and the new age was sure to pass it by. Maybe it was knowing that he'd never see old Johnny over there anymore. Louise had told him about old Johnny passing away. Castle wasn't surprised, not only because Johnny would have had to have been getting on to ninety and, what with his 'girl' May dead, life would have seemed meaningless. Johnny'd had a hell of a go, cowboy turned Wobbly-tough guy—that is until a gangster named Garmano pushed him off a bridge near Sedro Wooley. Johnny waited thirty years, thirty years of hauling junk around town with a kid's wagon, but he got even with Augie Garmano. And that's one of the reasons Castle wound up in Spain. But that's another story.

Rose was gone too. Fearless Rose, the anarchist pamphleteer. They'd been radicals in the nineteenth century, her and Johnny. It was a new era busting out all over.

Castle walked. People were in shirtsleeves and light dresses, enjoying the Indian summer. He took in the unusual sight of men carrying lunch pails. There was another unusual sight up ahead at the corner of Pender and Homer, a huge man who didn't seem to know or care that it was Indian summer, wearing a thick cap with ear muffs and a heavy overcoat, the hem of which was down around his shins. The overcoat was covered with medals and ribbons. So was the cap. When Castle was just a few yards away, he saw that it wasn't a very large man at all but a very large woman. Her face was round and red and glistening with sweat. She caught his eye and stared and without breaking the look, reached with her right hand to finger a medal on the left side of her chest. "I got this one for bravery at the Battle of Arbella when we crushed the Persians."

"You should be very proud."

"Not as proud as I am of this here with the blue ribbon."

She spoke in an inflectionless voice. "I was the only man survived Vimy Ridge. Went over the top with fifty other doughboys.

None of them made it. My best pal, he was right at my side, took a shell and exploded into thousands of pieces. My best pal. Just blood and gristle, and parts of him coming down on me like soft rain."

"I'm sorry. Goodbye."

"Goodbye."

There were two young women, maybe late-twenties coming toward him, with their hairdos and store packages, leaning their heads close and gossiping, giggling. A few seconds later, Castle looked over his shoulder and watched them pass within seven feet of the woman in the overcoat, thought of the greater distance that separated them.

The cigar store-newstand was on the northwest corner of the intersection of Pender and Granville where scads of people were rushing off in all directions. To the left, looking south up Granville, old buildings and telephone wires met in a perspective of pale blue sky; to the right, trolley tracks rolled down to the water; and across the Strait, the mountains sat waiting. He didn't know about the rest of the town's denizens but he never took those mountains for granted. Sure they were beautiful and had even been known to inspire him with awe but he wasn't about to sing them any odes and not because they were often brooding as hell and other times so oppressive he wanted to drink a gin joint dry. No, the damn things just stood there, had always been standing there, and would always be standing there—mocking, mocking the whole damn thing.

But knowing that didn't depress him; it may have bothered him but it didn't depress him. Castle just wasn't going to sing them any odes, no matter how they spoke to him. Nor pen them any panegyrics. There wasn't anything he could do about the damn mountains. Let's just keep things in perspective here. There was something he could do about Larry Sobell's obituaries.

There were lots of magazines and newspapers in the cigar store-newstand and plenty of cigar smoke too. The guy behind the counter had a cigar in his mug and so did the fellow on the other side of the counter facing him. They were puffing smoke and jawing about the brand new world-wide donnybrook. The man who didn't work in the store had a Racing Form in his left hand and was shaking it. "I agree with you whole-heartedly, we're rushing into this thing without thought. Great Britain says jump, and we jump. It's not our war."

"Damned right, it's not our war," growled the guy behind the counter. "And the Germans aren't our enemies. What they ever do to us? We shouldna fought them that last time either."

"Yes indeed," the other agreed, a fellow so thin, it looked like his suit had been draped over a young willow tree. His Adam's apple fluttered when he added a question, "Since when are the Poles any pals of ours, eh?"

The clerk nodded vigorous agreement, ash tumbling down onto the counter. He took the cigar out of his mouth. Castle—eavesdropping while ostensibly thumbing through a copy of *Ring Magazine*—noted that his lips seemed to be drooling. He jabbed the cigar like it was a dart and the other guy the board. "You think, if the Germans attacked Canada, the Poles would come over to help us out?"

Having scored his point, the man's sloppy lips rearranged themselves in a pleased smirk, and he turned and saw Castle looking at him, "You need some help?"

"If I do I'll let you know."

The man let his eyes dart from Castle's to the *Ring Magazine* and back, said, "This ain't the library, you know."

He had John L. Lewis eyebrows and his hair—there was something curious about the way he combed his hair—the two dark pompadours with a little white on the tops, like mounds, hell, like snow-covered mountains. The guy's head reminded Castle of the goddamned mountains on the other side of the Strait. That's what it was. He couldn't help grinning.

"I know it's not the library, the old ladies in there don't smoke cigars."

The man glowered at him. Castle changed his grin into a big smile and went over to the wall where the newspapers were displayed. There were the major dailies, the Chinese daily, out of town rags, sports sheets, suburban weeklies, and way down at the far end on the bottom, *The Jewish World.* Castle grabbed the last copy, stuck it under his arm, took an envelope from his inside pocket, removed an obit, opened the paper and was checking his clipping against the *World's* obituary section when the counterman said, "What'd you think you're doing?"

Castle didn't answer. He put the stuff back in his pocket, and came toward the counter with the paper. Placed a nickel on the counter. The guy looked at the name of the paper and gave Castle a hard stare.

"It doesn't work," Castle said.

"Huh?"

"Your tough guy look. It might work on the ones that come in here for *Crocheting Weekly* but not on us readers of *The Jewish World*."

The man looked confused. Castle reached for the door knob. As he was going out, he heard the clerk mutter to the other cigar, "Goddamn kikes. We should fight for them?"

Castle walked west to Howe Street, turned south and headed up to Georgia Street. Near the corner on the other side, out front of an office building, was a long, sleek and gun-metal grey Cadillac, laden with chrome. He looked at the shiny bumper, thinking about how the bumpers on his decrepit Nash didn't mirror cornices and gargoyles, bricks and pale blue sky like that. He'd have to go and pay the Nash a visit; to hell with extras like bumpers that mirrored the sky, he just hoped the rattletrap would still run.

Castle heard his name and only had to move his gaze a few feet from the bumper to locate the caller. Well it was actually more like ten feet given the length of the machine. The man doing the calling was the driver, Raymond Thomas, Negro buddy of Guy Roberts, the sugar king. There was a another Negro standing by the driver's door. This one looked over too, nodded at Raymond, and started up the street.

Castle crossed Howe, came up to the car.

"Hey, Raymond. I like your cap. Car's not bad either."

Raymond fingered the brim, "Thank you, Massa. You know I got to wear this thing though it makes me feel like I should be on a yacht."

"Well looking at this baby, I can see how you'd feel that way."

"Yeah, Guy and I bought it a couple of months ago. Thirty-nine Cadillac. Had to purchase the cap the next day, the way people looked at me. You know when I'm parked at the curb waiting for Guy. Like I am now."

"It goes well with your hundred and fifty dollar suit."

"Thanks. I acquired the cap in a sporting goods store that caters to the sailing crowd. You ever try shopping for such a thing, telling sales clerks you want a chaffeur's cap?"

"Sure I have Raymond but it's been awhile."

"Might be a good little business to get into, chaffeur uniforms. Butler, maid, valet outfits. What with the economy improving. Imagine that, eh? My family going from domestic uniforms to domestic uniforms in two generations."

"Save it for the sob sisters, Raymond. Your folks owned a plantation over there on Saltspring. You had domestic help to give orders to. Unfortunate Samoans or something who called you 'Massa.'"

"Hawaiians. Sandwich Islanders we called them."

Thomas made a show of looking around with a worried expression.

"But let us not speak about that in public, Castle. I got to keep my little game going. But speaking of business, I wonder if you would be interested in taking on a little assignment for me. If you don't mind working for me that is. If you know what I mean."

"You mean, because you're of the dusky persuasion? What the newspapers like to call an Ethiopian? You know me, Raymond. Situations such as this, I don't see an Ethiopian, I see a client."

"You can trowel it on almost as smooth as me," Raymond Thomas said, shaking his head appreciatively.

"A big compliment. What's the deal?"

"Nothing much. Just a company we're thinking of investing in."

Thomas held up the paper he had been studying, called the Financial Report, took a mechanical pencil from his jacket pocket, circled a name in a column. "Byerstock Investments. Catchy name, eh? Buy Our Stock?"

He held the paper up and Castle looked at the name, looked at

Thomas' fingers, long and medium-brown like those cigars, Imperials. The nails were the colour of old ivory and as shiny as the bumper of the Cadillac.

"Figures look good but we don't know anything about the folks in charge."

"That worry you?"

"Not at all. They could be new kids on the block or just out of town fellows or some locals who don't want to make any big promoting noise. It's just that Guy and I have so many things on the fire now there's no time to do the usual research. What's your fee?"

"We can talk about that later. It's not my field, you know, so I can't promise anything."

"Might be a good one for you to get into though, way things are going. Yes sir, I believe that there is opportunity knocking for you."

"Yeah, and as usual I won't answer. Too mysterious for me, the world of business."

"And you an old carney."

"That was just simple straight-forward chicanery."

"I tell you what, Gene. I got some money, most of the money, in a new club just opened over on Homer Street. Afterhours place called Porters' Retreat. They hired a girl singer couple days ago and she sounds like a combination of Lee Wiley and this Billie Holiday. Musicians tell me she's as good as either."

"That's hard to believe."

"Yeah, hard to believe she's white too. Or almost. Half-Gypsy or something. Don't know what colour that makes her. And playing in back of her is a quintet of fun-loving Ethiopians. Why don't you and the lovely Louise fall by this week as my guests? You can let me know if you've discovered anything."

"Sounds good, Raymond. See you then."

CHAPTER FOUR

Castle turned right at Georgia and had to stop for traffic at the corner of Burrard, the jazz corner. There was the Palomar Supper Club with a sign in the window bidding him come dine and dance to the madcap rhythms of the ten-piece Frankie DeFrancis band. And up on top of the latest edition of the Hotel Vancouver, in the rooftop lounge, another orchestra for dining and dancing. He imagined the sons and daughters of doctors and lawyers over in West Vancouver or out in Kitsilano, piling into roadsters and waving pennants during the ride into town, piling out and rushing into the Palomar or up to the Rooftop Lounge to go wild—absolutely bonkers!—foxtrotting to the happy-go-lucky sounds of bands who were proud of sounding like Glen Gray or, heaven's to Betsy, Paul Whiteman.

There was also the post office. Castle went in the big doors and stood at one of the high counters where guys were licking stamps. He gave the place a slant. There were men behind windows with grills that put him in mind of priests and confessionals, and one priest was a guy he knew; a fact that was a big surprise considering the guy.

"Could this here be a fella of my acquaintance called Ernie Elway?" Castle said, stepping up.

"Yeah, the same. How you been, Gene Castle?"

Ernie Elway had blond hair parted in the middle and a little moustache so pale you weren't sure it was there.

"I'm fine, Ernie but the last I heard you were in this same post office only you were sitting down with a picket sign and refusing to budge."

"Shhh!" Ernie glanced to his left and glanced to his right. "They don't know about that. What you didn't hear was that I got up off the floor and ran out of the building on account of the cops let loose the tear gas on us."

"Where'd you run to?"

"I guess you could say I ran all the way to the employment office, got this job and came humbly back. So what can I do for you?"

Castle put down one of Sobell's envelopes.

"You could tell me what this little line means on the postmark. I know other postmarks have them in other places. Just one per postmark."

"Yeah, that's right. In this town, the way it works, all mail goes through four postal stations. The lines indicate the stations."

"Kind of figured something like that."

"Yeah. This is the main station and if the mail starts out here, it is marked with a little line jutting down from where twelve o'clock would be. Hastings and Nanaimo is three o'clock, 41st and Fraser six o'clock, and this one here that you got, nine o'clock, was posted at Tenth and Macdonald."

"Thanks, I appreciate it. Say, Ernie. You miss the old days, fighting for justice and freedom?"

"Yeah, I sure do Gene. It was exciting. But there isn't much future in that sort of thing on this side of the ocean is there? I mean justice and freedom. A guy's got to be realistic."

"I know what you mean. See you around, Ernie."

Castle walked back to Burrard Street where there was a bus stop. There was no bus in sight so he fought his way inside a telephone booth and fought his way out again after he'd called the offices of *The Jewish World* and learned that their sheet went out on the trucks early enough to be at all distribution outlets by noon every Thursday.

Castle rode the bus to Broadway and transferred to another one going west. Every block took him deeper into strange territory, strange for him because it seemed so tranquil after the streets of downtown. Big old wooden houses and little stucco ones on a Southern California theme. Lawns with old trees and shrubbery too. Flowers on some hydrangea bushes still had colour to them even though October had reached middle-age. He liked hydrangea bushes, Castle did, and azaleas, especially the big ones, and verburum wasn't bad. He would have liked forsythias too only they made a big show and were gone all too quickly, sort of like a cheap romance. It happens in March, a burst of beautiful, heartbreaking yellow but just as suddenly as she appeared, she's gone. Could be a woman's name. Forysthia. Yellow like that shoe, come to think of it, the heel of which had been imbedded in the skull of Moncrieff Dilman.

What the hell brought that on? Castle asked himself as he looked out the windows at a young woman pushing a baby carriage. As the bus wheezed by, he was just able to make out a couple of pudgy cheeks amidst the swaddling clothes. What kind of world will that kid inherit? Probably live into the next century. And he can have it. Of course, it is possible that I could live to the next century. Not bloodly likely but humanly possible. I'd be—what?—one hundred and four? No thanks. What a terrible imposition that would be. I wouldn't be able to climb those stairs, have to get an office on the ground floor.

The man at the Macdonald Postal Depot probably wasn't one hundred and four but he looked to be closing in on it. He was bald, his skin the colour of old paper like on historical documents such as you'd see in a museum. Like the ones they had over in Victoria, those treaties they got the local indians to sign, telling them they'd honour forever and forever, and then went back to Government House, had a few drinks and laughed at the naivete of the savages.

The old man sat silent and still, watching Castle walk toward him across the marble floor. Castle watched back. There was no one else around. The man still wore a detachable collar like Larry Sobell's father used to sell. He looked like he needed help putting his on. Up close the old man reminded him of one of those heads carved on the bowl of a pipe you bought in Austria. His eyes were the palest, palest blue, just a hint of the tint of blue.

"Howdy, young fellow, what can I do for you?"

Castle almost jumped at the voice. It was like the pipe bowl started talking to you.

The face rearranged itself into a wide smile of yellow teeth.

"Stamps, money order, penny postcards, special delivery. You name it, we got it."

"I need some advice."

"I'll do my best, young man. I'm Dad Durkens representing the Canadian Postal Service, and I'm at your service."

"Thanks, Dad."

"You know, I don't believe I've seen you around here before."

"Don't get to these parts much."

"Nope. Didn't think so. I know most people that come in here. And most people who walk past the windows. I just sit here and watch."

"Why that's just fine, Dad, on account of what I have in mind. I wonder if you have many persons, I'm speaking of regulars, who come in every Thursday afternoon to mail letters. Probably not too long after noon, early enough anyway to get a letter postmarked the same day."

"There's no telling who's liable to come in and mail a letter, you know. Life is so unpredictable which is what makes it so interesting, don't you think?"

"I agree entirely, Dad."

"Yes, sir. Variety is not only the spice of life but it is the very—what you call it?—essence of existence. Do you realize all of evolution is based on diversity?"

"Now that you mention it, Dad, it figures."

"Species would stagnant and die were it not for diversity. Why just yesterday afternoon which was Thursday, of course, a lady I'd never seen before came in with a big package. Carrying it in front of her, couldn't even see over the top, had to peek around it, real comical-like, cause her little hat fell off. One of those pill box jobs. Why was she at my postal station? Been thinking of her ever since. Had nice slender ankles on her, too."

"You don't miss a trick then do you?"

"No, sir. Got two regulars come in here every Thursday, early afternoon. One is Mrs. Dixon with all her contest entries. She clips the coupons out of magazines and newspapers and sends them in.

Twenty or thirty every week. Win a year's supply of Oleo Margarine, free admittance all summer long to Jericho Beach Pavillion. That kind of thing. Must be looking for another husband on account of she always goes dancing at the Pavillion. First husband was killed in the last set-to over to Europe. I was too old for that one. Hell, I was too old for the Boer War or even that Franco-Prussian do. Now, Mrs. Dixon's getting on but she's got spunk to spare. I like spunk in a woman. You?"

"Spunk can make up for a lot, Dad. What about the other regular?"

"That'd be young Mr. Fremont. Never see him in here except on Thursdays, one-thirty, religious. The way I figure, he stops in after lunch. Been doing it about three months. Don't say nothing except every couple weeks, a 'Howdoin?'. He's also nodded a few times. Usually just struts over to the slot, sticks in his one letter, turns and leaves, goes back to the garage. Mrs. Dixon, she hands her bunch of letters to me. Everyone's got their own style of doing things. But young Mr. Fremont he can't be any mechanic that fellow because he's always dressed in a spiffy suit and tie, usually a hat. Must think he's some kind of gangster. Jimmy Cagney, maybe."

"The way you describe him puts me in mind of a fellow of my aquaintance also named Fremont. Guy who wishes he was a gangster, Eddie Fremont."

"The one used to be a not bad lightweight prizefighter?"

"That's right, Dad."

"Saw him take on Gordy Lawton at the Point Roberts Barn, back in '29. Took a split decision. Why, I'm a solid fan of pugilism. Always have been. How about you, son?"

"Since a kid."

"Well you were just a kid when I was in attendance that day back in March ought-nine in our own hometown when the great Jack Johnson made his first defense of the title he won from Tiny Tommy Burns. The other guy became a screen actor and even won one of them Academy Awards a few years back. Victor McLaglen."

"Was it the farce I've heard it was?"

"It was entertaining for sure. Jack put him down in the first and McLaglen was out for about thirty seconds but they let him continue so the crowd would think it got its money's worth."

"So, Eddie Fremont?"

"The one comes in here is his younger brother, name of Cyril."

"You go over to the box behind the slot, gather up the letters and mark them?"

"Cancelling the stamps. That's part of my job."

Castle showed Dad Durkens a few of the letters. The old man nodded his head.

"Those are the ones. No doubt about it. I got a memory for these kinds of things. A young man's memory and zest for life."

"You sure seem to, and that's a fact. Would you happen to know where this garage is?"

"'Deed I do. Just four blocks down Tenth Avenue, going west."

"Okay. Thanks again, Dad."

"Say, why you looking for this young Mr. Fremont? You're not a cop."

"You're right. It's just that his Thursday mailings wind up annoying a friend of mine."

"This Mr. Sobell?"

"Damn, Dad. You're on the earie with both eyes open. How old are you, you don't mind my asking?"

"I'm ninety-one but don't tell the postal department authorities. Ninety-one and I still got lead in my pencil."

"Good for you but it's Mrs. Dixon you ought to tell that to."

"I already have, son." Dad Durkens winked at Castle. "Yes, indeedy, I already have."

Castle told him goodbye and said he'd see him around. Dad gave a little wave and reverted to his museum stillness. Ninety-one. One hundred and four. It's possible."

Castle strolled down Tenth, had a gander at the garage in question, Ralph's Repair, and battled another phone booth for the purpose of calling his client. He told Sobell he'd found the sender and the first thing Sobell did was express amazement that Castle had done the job so quickly. Sobell was saying how much he appreciated it when he remembered to ask the name of the sender. When Castle told him,

Sobell sounded perplexed, said he didn't know anybody named Cyril Fremont and started trying to renege on all the nice things he'd said. Castle remarked that there couldn't be any doubt and is this it or are you curious. Sobell was curious and Castle said okay, but, of course, it will cost you some more moo-la. Sobell went, Yeah, yeah. Just get it done. And now Castle was walking across the street to the garage.

There were all those big, handsome wooden houses and neat Southern California bungalows, clean and tidy outside, and the people who mowed the lawns and clipped the hedges managed to do so without getting dirty. But one step was all it took to enter another world. Inside, everything that wasn't greasy was getting that way. There were two pits and a lift. A greasy door in the far wall. He could make out the grimey sleeves of a set of overalls in one of the pits under a four-door Ford sedan and the entire grimey overall uniform of a man under a Desoto that was up on the lift. This man's uniform was baggy at his legs but stretched tight across his belly. He was no more than forty. What hair he had left was long and black but the fellow's hairline had reached the top of his crown and seemed poised for a mad ride down the other side. He had grease streaks on his forehead from brushing away loose strands. He was back by the universal joint making ratchety-ratchet sounds with his ratchet wrench. A few feet away from him was a wooden chest about four feet high on wheels with drawers of tools and more tools on the top. He looked up, saw Castle. "Yeah? What'd you want?"

"I got an old Nash been up on blocks for three years. Want to get it checked out before I license it. You want to give it a going over?"

"You get it here, I'll look it over. But not for a couple days. I'm busy."

"That'll be fine."

In the corner to the left of the entrance, Castle noticed a little office had been partitioned off from the rest of the garage. The windows were smudged and everything in the office was dirty. There was a desk in there covered with bills and auto manuals and a hubcap filled with cigarette butts. There was grease on the cigarette butts. Not the kind of place for a dapper dude in a suit and fedora.

"Something else you want?"

"Oh, I was just thinking this is not the kind of place you expect to find a vined-down fellow like Cyril Fremont."

"Who?"

"Cyril Fremont. You know him, he's the only guy who works out of here doesn't wear those cute overalls."

"I think it's time you get out of here, pal."

"No. I don't think so. Not yet."

The mechanic put the ratchet down on top of the tool chest, exchanged it for an open-ended wrench about two feet long, and looked menacingly at Castle.

"Golly, that one's dirty too. You ought to clean this place up a bit."

"I'm gonna clean you up, pal. You don't vamoose out of here."

"The way you're acting, you'd think Cyril doesn't have any friends, only people who don't like him coming to do him harm. I may be his long lost buddy for all you know."

To his left Castle heard something metal fall to the cement, and looked to see the other guy in overalls climbing up the cement steps of the grease pit.

"What's the problem, Bart?"

"Hey, Bob. Told this punk here to leave but he doesn't get the message."

The new man was younger, lankier, looked to be in decent shape, moved well as he closed the space between them. "Maybe we ought to give him the message a little louder," the young guy said, and picked a tire iron off the ground.

"You better beat it, pal," Bart advised, coming closer. "You know what's good for you."

"No, I still don't think so."

"You're crazy. You don't have a chance."

"Oh, indeed I do."

Castle raised his right leg and took the knife from the sheath under his sock, held it up. Bob replied by banging the tire iron down hard on a work bench.

"You thought that would make me drop the knife? Think I don't know how to use this? Come and find out. What I'm going to do is, I'm going to throw it at you, Bob. It's not really a thower, it's a fighting knife but, what the hell, it'll do. Four inch blade going right in under your breast bone. Then with you dying there on the dirty concrete, all I got to do is handle Bart here. I don't need a blade for that because Bart is overweight and slow, and deep down isn't inclined to tangle, ain't that right, Bart?"

In the instant just before Bart was coming to the conclusion that Castle was indeed correct, another voice intruded, loudly inquiring, "Fuck's going on here?"

The man was wearing a tan linen suit, brown knit tie, brown and white shoes. Had one hand on the inside knob of the door in the rear wall.

Bart, making up for his hesitation, answered in his gruff voice, "Guy here snooping around. Doesn't want to leave."

"Hi there, Cyril. It's Gene Castle, old friend of your brother's."

"Gene Castle?" Cyril leaned to his right to get a look, still holding on to the knob, holding the rest of him still. Probably, Castle thought, reluctant to move and maybe get his suit dirty. Castle didn't blame him.

"Oh, yeah. Gene Castle. I recognize you from your picture in the paper a few years back. What do you want?"

"Just want to talk with you a minute or two."

"I should have one of my boys with me?"

"No, you don't need either of them."

"I don't know. You asked my brother a few questions once and messed him up a bit."

"Messed up the knot in his tie was all I did. Bought him a drink and gave him a double sawbuck too."

"I don't drink but maybe you could also slip me a double sawbuck."

"Probably could."

"Come on back."

"First, send the one monkey back in his pit and the other one, bad Bart there, I got to walk near him to get to you and I'm keeping the blade in my hand all the way."

"You won't need it cause Bart won't do anything."

Castle came forward and Bart found something that needed his attention in the vicinity of the universal joint.

Cyril held the door for Castle who decided the guy wouldn't

move on him even if he didn't have the blade in his hand. He passed into a room in which there were wooden crates and cardboard boxes which surely held stolen goods just like the stolen goods that were scattered and stacked all around. There were electric fans, bicycles, golf clubs and washing machines; there were cabinet radios and Victrolas, rifles and shotguns, floor lamps, adding machines and typewriters. There was a rollup door that the trucks backed up to in order to load and unload the stuff. There was a side door in the conventional mode that gave on to the alley in case the cops came calling of an evening.

"Nice operation you got, Cyril," Castle said, returning the knife to its hiding place.

"I don't got it, I just run it," the dapper man grunted. "But how come you know me and where to find me?"

Castle had exchanged the blade for the envelopes which he handed to Fremont.

Cyril flipped through them, smirked.

"So why you want to scare an old fat man sending these every week?"

"I never knew what was in them. What're they anyway?"

"Obituaries."

"Obituaries?"

"You know, it's what they put in the paper when you die, if the paper thinks you warrant such a thing or if your loved ones want to pay for it."

"I just do it for a guy."

"What guy?"

"Guy that runs this operation."

"He got a name?"

"I forgot it."

Castle took out his billfold, took out a double sawbuck, held it out.

"I remember it," Fremont said. "Sherman Redman."

"So this Sherman Redman gives you an envelope every Thursday to run down the street and mail? So what are you, his errand boy?"

Fremont grimaced, "Yeah, looks like. I mean, I'm doing all right here but this Redman, I should never of gotten mixed up with him."

"How did you get involved?"

"My dear sweet big brother."

"And how is the former contender?"

"He's shaking a jolt in Glenora. Three to seven for armed robbery."

"That's not too heavy a bit though I wouldn't have thought guns were his style."

"They ain't, I mean that ain't his nature, but he developed a serious Jones. And in a way you had a lot to do with it."

"Me? When was this? I been out of town."

"Yeah, it was not too long after you left town. After the big scandal with the chief of police and the Garmano gang. My brother told me all about it. He made out pretty good off of that. Used to say,'That Castle, he don't have any idea what he put me on to.'"

"What'd I put him on to? The last I saw him, Eddie was afraid of what I might have put on *to* him. The Italians finding out he provided me with the key to the whole thing."

"No, that big bust busted up the dagos and for a couple of months it was like the goddamn Klondike around here. People coming over the pass and up the river for a chance at the spoils. Well Eddie sifted through the tailings, so to speak, picked up on some of the dirty pictures-blue movie action what Garmano had going and made himself some long green. He'd started chippying horse and pretty soon the monkey got on his back. Then my brother got sloppy. Sloppy in his actions, sloppy in the way he looked."

"Hard to imagine, your brother turning out sloppy."

"Yeah," Cyril, shook his head as if at a nightmarish reminder, tugged his lapels. "Me, I don't mess with the drugs or booze either. I don't want to wind up like that. You think I resemble my brother?"

"You look like him only you don't dye your hair. You don't mind me saying it, your brother was a little too, well, he was obvious like. I mean, a guy with shoe polish black hair, you're concentrating on that while he's running down his game. So right there, Eddie was encumbered from the get-go."

"Was what?"

"He always went up to the plate with the count o and one.

Pressure was on him so he had to force the action, if you get my drift."

"Yeah, I do. I don't take offense neither. I'm planning my career, you understand. I don't need to make enemies unnecessarily. Way I figure I'll make enough anyway."

"This Sherman Redman. You talk like he's a potential enemy."

"Yeah, maybe he is."

"What's he involved in?"

"A little this, a little that. He's got this here insurance scam going that I get a cut out of. Out of what I fence from here. That kind of thing. That's how my brother got involved with him, doing those insurance capers. He's got some twisted buddy likes to burn places down. Owners get the insurance money and split it. And it was my brother hepped him to the dirty movies and pictures, and Redman put up some dough to get that going. Took it over when Eddie got sent up."

"He ever say what he has against this Larry Sobell that you send the letters too?"

Cyril shrugged. "He never said nothing about him. I never asked."

"All right. I'll be seeing you. Never know when we might do a little business again."

"I laid some interesting details on you, Castle. It ought to be worth another double sawbuck."

"Naw, it's worth a single double sawbuck."

Fremont shrugged again but Castle handed it over.

"What about the grease monkies? What'd they do?"

"Go out on the capers at night, work on the cars during the day. That's how we launder the money, through the garage."

"You ought to launder those galoots. They must leave grease prints at the scene of the crime."

"We cover em with Jet Bon Ami, hose em down before a job."

"This door lead to the alley? I think I'll take it. Got a feeling young Bob out there has a hankering to try something and I don't want to stick the blade in him."

"You can use that shiv?"

"Use to throw a little in the carney. Fellow has a blade and can't or won't use it, he's going be in trouble eventually."

"Been good doing business with you."

Castle went out into the alley.

Back downtown, he was surprised to find it was still early afternoon. Castle'd only been to the Kitsilano area of town, half an hour away on two buses including the wait between, yet it seemed like a journey into terra icognita. It had been a good trip though, him bringing back the week's nut. But it won't do to rest on your laurels, Castle told himself.

So he took himself to the Public Library and got the Company Directory from a balding middle-aged man who wore braces and a red bowtie. There weren't only little ladies in there, and none of the help smoked cigars, unless they did so on their breaks. The bowtied fellow glided back to a desk he shared with a middle-aged woman whose hair was pulled back in a bun. Castle hadn't been in a library for a long time but it seemed to him that all lady librarians wore their hair in buns. Maybe it was required.

Castle discovered that Byerstock Investments had been founded in 1937 and its director was somebody called Gus Tod. There were no Tods in the telephone book and only a few Todds but nobody named Gus, or with G. as a first or middle initial. Maybe Gus slept at the office. The Company Directory indicated Byerstock's initial capitalization and noted that it had a few small real estate holdings, unspecified, but was mostly involved in import-export and mining ventures. All of this Castle copied in a little brown notebook with a yellow stub of pencil.

As he put the notebook away, Castle noticed out of the corner of his eye that the fellow with the bowtie and the lady with the bun were discussing him between glances. Although they were all the way across the floor and talking to themselves, Castle knew what they were saying. He hadn't wasted all those years in the carnivals afterall. A little lip reading, a smidgen of knife throwing and some talking the front were just three of the skills with which he had some aquaintance. He didn't, however, imagine that'd make much of an impression on a job application. On the other hand, he had never actually applied for a job. Sure, he'd signed up to fight in places like France, Nicaragua, Ethiopia and Spain but since he could walk and talk, they'd taken him. They took anybody they could get.

So when Castle looked slantwise, he caught the middle-aged woman telling the guy, "I think he's sort of, well, one wouldn't call him handsome..."

The guy interjecting, "One certainly would not."

The woman completing her thought, "but he is interesting looking."

The bow-tie guy, rolling his eyes, saying, "He's too—how should I put it?—used or weathered for my tastes."

Castle got up, telling himself he should leave in case the fellow changed his mind.

CHAPTER FIVE

He felt better for visiting the library and decided it was now all right to rest on his laurels. He was a bit peckish and could also use a beer or two. The Seaman's Club was a good place to have them, six-seven blocks away, give him a chance to smoke the town over a bit. Afterall, he'd spent most of his three days back cuddled up with Louise, listening to ships' whistles, sipping from one bottle and another, watching the sky change colours outside the hotel room window and the red neon sign come to life late every day between the afternoon and the night. That was his favourite time, Louise's favourite time. They looked up the name once: crepuscular. They loved the crepuscular time. But the best of all crepuscular times was when the two of you were in bed and it came around. You could be on your own though, out on deck of a boat, leaning on the rail. Like just a couple of weeks ago—could it be only a couple of weeks?—coming back from Europe. He really had slept in his clothes in a cheap room in one of those alleys six blocks off the Canebiere, and when the alarm went off, hit the deck arunning, grabbing his bag and making for the fishing boat in the old port. The big ships didn't come into the old port any more and the new port was to hell and gone, and he wasn't about to try and board anything there anyway. So they went out to that island thirty miles off, and naturally he couldn't help thinking of it as Monte Cristo, and him the Count making his escape. And there he was that very early evening looking back at Europe, at Spain, even more than France, watching it fade away in the crepuscular time.

But in the time of mid-October, the streets were filled because everybody knew it was the sunshine's last gasp, and the bleak and the wet were at any moment going to claim the stage from this bright usurper. Shoppers, and kids marching off to war, and old Aarno Kranjola sitting under the Birk's Clock drawing portraits with colour sticks in his block-like hands; Aarno, his massive skull and forehead split by a wide scar from which erupted tufts of hair. He looked like a killer from the chaingang swamps until he smiled that Shirley Temple smile.

The Seaman's Club was over Goody's Goods, a store that sold clothes and supplies to the working man. Not to your trolley drivers or production line slaves, though they wouldn't be turned down should they wish to purchase caulk boots, peaveys or hip waders. Castle didn't need any of those items but used to like to stop in and trade howdies with Goody who hadn't been up to doing a lick of work for fifteen years at least, ever since he took sick which is what lead him to open the store. Goody figured that after working on the boats and in the bush for so long, he had enough friends and aquaintances to keep him going. Goody had known Castle's old man when Goody was a young man and the old man was old. If the old man was still around, he might be like one of the characters Castle'd see in the store, eighty-year old Svenskas pawing the boots, the lined flannel shirts, stagging their new britches right there at the counter, muttering about how easy the bush monkies had it these days.

But Castle could see Goody in there putting a rain slicker in a box, hacking, taking money, covering his mouth to cough, handing over change with the same hand, so he opened the other door and walked upstairs to the Seaman's Club.

Two sides of the club were taken over by windows that looked out onto Richards Street and the laneway, the bar and server's area cut into a wall that was surrounded by photographs of ships, the fourth wall had built-in fish tanks with tropical fish in them. Between the alley windows and the end of the fish tank wall was an alcove six feet long that lead to washrooms, and the alcove served as a monument to all the old seamen who had gone to Davey Jones' locker. Their photographs were there, their seaman's cards were there. You thought of them every time you went to pee.

Castle took a seat by himself at one of the round tables. The place looked strange with sunlight coming in the windows. It would be at its best any day now with blinds pulled down, rain like chattering teeth on the windows, the furnace going full blast and Matty Muldoon leaning across the table with a conspiratorial air. As it was, his story this afternoon was filled with sunlight, him and his mates anchored somewhere off Madagascar or the Maldives, someplace where the ocean was turquoise and the sand white and the natives were rowing out in two canoes. There were three fellows at the table with Matty, hanging on his words, "Yessir, and who do you think was filling up them canoes? Except for the two fellows paddling, one in each canoe, it was all lovely brown-skinned girls and they didn't have nothing on up top. No sir, just this thick wavy black hair that hung down and now it covers those pretty little things and now it don't. Well, me hardies, I was nineteen years old..."

Just as the first girl was halfway up the rope ladder, Castle felt a hand on his shoulder and looked up to see Joe Frontenac, fedora pushed back at a rakish angle on his dark tousled hair. Joe displayed his perfect white teeth, his dark eyes ablaze as they always were. A handsome devil in rumpled clothes. The way the guy dressed it was as if he had a wife who bought him ill-fitting duds that she never ironed on account of maybe this would lessen his appeal to other woman. But Joe was single and never thought about clothes.

He told Castle it was really great to see him, and the reporter meant it too. And Castle replied in kind. They'd gone through a lot together, starting with a case in Vancouver years before and continuing through several months' worth of adventure in Spain. But they hadn't seen each other for a couple of years now, so they clapped each other on the back and ordered drinks, and got to cutting up touches.

It must have been nearly an hour later, that Frontenac asked Castle what he was doing in the Seaman's Club, and Castle said, "Why I was just about to hear about what happened when nineteen year old Matty Muldoon met ten or twelve beautiful half-naked women when you came over and interrupted."

Frontenac looked over his shoulder.

"Matty's the one with the face the colour of a lobster," Castle said. "He's over eighty, spent most of those years at sea. Now he makes the rounds from Ramona's to the club here and winds up at night in the Anchor Tavern."

"What a mug on the guy. He must have some stories, eh?"

"A million of them. So what're you doing?"

"On the prowl for stories."

"Well there you go. Do a series on Matty there. Only you'd have to change your billing. Couldn't call the column, 'I Was There,' have to change it to 'He Was There.'"

"That might be a good idea. It would also show that I'm a humble sort of fellow."

"That's what I've always liked about you, Joe. Daredevil Ace Reporter you may be, but you're shot through with touching humility."

"Thanks. By the way, I flashed my press card but how did you get in here?"

"I'm an old salt, didn't you know? Well a middle-aged salt. Used to ship out during all those carnival off-seasons. You could catch a ship fairly easy out of here after the war, the last war, and in the early twenties. Or maybe if we went to winter quarters some place near Tampa or Galveston, I'd grab something there."

"You're full of surprises."

"Part of my charm."

"You working on anything?"

"Already finished one job and started on another. Which reminds me, before I bid bye-bye to the first one, you ever hear of a guy called Sherman Redman, who is not a legitimate operator?"

The reporter took off his fedora and ran a hand through his thick locks, Castle thinking the guy should do ads for how healthy your hair will look after shampooing with Prel or something. An insouciant, roguishly handsome devil, was Joe Frontenac; too bad he was only five foot five. Hell, maybe it was just as well that he wasn't any taller. Think of all the mischief he'd get up to if he was five feet eleven. Or maybe Castle was just envious.

"No. No I don't think so."

"But, something?"

Frontenac shook his head, "It somehow seemed familiar for a moment, but, no, I don't come up with anything."

"Keep it in mind."

"Will do. Say, I did a piece on Rose Jenkins' funeral. They ran pictures with it."

"I'd like to see it."

"Oh, yeah and Rose left you something in her will. Her scrapbook."

"That's mighty fine. I'll treasure that. Her and the doc in the old days. Lot of history in there, I bet. Can't wait to see it."

"Her grandson is holding it for you. He came out for the funeral and stayed. He's in his late twenties. Jerry Fraser's his name."

"Is he like his grandmother?"

"Not in any way that I can tell. He reminds me of one of those guys you find at the race track with their tip sheets and pamphlets about this or that sure-fire system for beating the odds and retiring to Florida. Some of those people, I did a story on them once, they are serious students with filing systems and their apartments are littered with papers. Only Jerry doesn't play the track, he plays the stock market and puts out a sort of tip sheet called the Financial Report for guys who want to make a million betting on the Bourse instead of a horse."

"You're right, he doesn't sound like Rose. But he sounds like a guy I want to meet."

"I'll give you his address. You introduce me to Matty Muldoon."

"Deal."

"This Jerry Fraser you go up to his flat, it's his grandmother's old place, he works out of there, he has a poster of Rose's on his bathroom wall. It's a picture of that guy Proudhon with his famous quote on it, you know the one."

"Yeah, 'Property is Theft.'"

"Jerry has it up there he says for its ironic value."

"Let's go see Matty Muldoon. Then I got to meet Louise. Remember to find out what happened with the dark-skinned girls."

CHAPTER SIX

Louise was lying on the bed, reading from a sheaf of papers. Castle skimmed his hat toward the chair near the window, missed, and the hat almost sailed out into the wild blue yonder.

"Nice shot," Louise said. "The neon sign would have looked jaunty with a fedora propped on top."

"Uh huh. And what's this we have here?"

"This? This is a girl on the kip in a slip with a script."

"You got the part?"

"Un huh. Had to do a cold reading. It's an Armed Services variety show. We'll be going around to bases putting it on. Little skits, song and dance routines. Yeah," Louise smirked "If this turns out not to be a phoney war afterall, I could have some long term employment."

"When do you leave town, sweetheart?"

"Oh, Gene. I hate to tell you. Two days."

"Two days?"

"Yeah, but, look, baby. I don't have to take it. I mean, you just got back. We haven't hardly seen each other and..."

"No, you do have to take it, Louise. Think of all those days without walking the boards. Remember the Depression. It seems like just yesterday."

"You're my guy, Gene. And, oh, tomorrow, we're doing a little sample of the review on the radio. A CBC nation-wide hookup."

"Great, kid. Let's celebrate. Go out to the new restaurant they got in Stanley Park that overlooks Lost Lagoon. Candlelight. Watch the swans. Soft music playing."

"Sounds very romantic. Then we can rush back here in a taxi and I'll model some of the skimpy outfits they gave me for the show. You know, I'll put 'em on me and you take 'em off me."

"Good. I hope they gave you a lot of outfits. I mean I might not see you for awhile and it's liable to be a long war."

It wasn't easy rolling out of bed early the next morning but Castle's partner in the night's escapades was there to share the morning's misery. Louise had rehearsals at nine so they acted like responsible people and were on the street by eight o'clock. At Ramona's, Louise sipped coffee and nibbled on toast while Castle attacked a stack of four. Guy Roberts and Raymond Thomas nodded to them from their usual places on stools at the counter and, later, while Roberts paid the cheque, Thomas came over, holding his chaffeur's cap in one hand, and offered his good mornings. "We're going over to Victoria for a couple of days on some business, but I'll be back at the end of the week Go by the place I was telling you about, Gene. The Porters' Retreat."

"Sounds good, Raymond. See you then."

Raymond Thomas walked away, putting on the cap. Guy Roberts was waiting by the cash register and opened the door for his chaffeur. Castle watched Louise watching them. She looked back at him. He said, "I know what you're thinking."

"You don't think that...?"

Castle shrugged, "Anything's possible, kid, in these topsy-turvy times."

"Yeah," Louise nodded. "My contacts in the industry tell me Cary Grant hops into the sack with Randy Scott. Can you believe it?"

"Starting six weeks ago, I can believe anything."

"Why what happened then?"

"That's when Joe Stalin climbed into bed with Adolph Hitler."

"I bet that didn't do anything for Party Membership."

"No, all over Europe, one saw dazed functionaries staggering in the streets wondering what had hit them, and when could they get a boat to New York. And speaking of Party hacks, whatever happened to our old pal, Martin Finnegan?"

"Why, you want his address so you can send him an I-told-you-so card?"

"That's a thought. No, I just wish him well."

"He'd left town by the time I got back late in '37. Heard rumours he's a spy in Ottawa."

"Maybe he plants false information with Mackenzie King. Uses our addle-brained prime minister's pooch as the medium. Hey, that's not a bad idea for one of your radio plays."

"Which reminds me," Louise said, getting up from the booth. "I probably shouldn't be late for the first rehearsal."

"You don't like the idea, eh?"

"What?"

"The three-hander. King, a sultry spy like yourself and a pooch."

"Work on it."

"See you, doll."

"Glad you liked the outfits," Louise flung that over her shoulder, added some extra emphasis to her hips and was out Ramona's door, whoever Ramona was.

When Jerry Fraser let him into his grandmother's old apartment on Jackson Street, Castle immediately began to take everything in, make comparisons. It wasn't as surprising as it was disconcerting. Not finding much family resemblance between grandmother and grandson, Castle supposed he was looking for it in the apartment. Jerry's grandmother used to wear her hair pulled back and gathered in a ring that always reminded Castle of one of those circular neon lighting tubes. She wore long dresses and stout shoes, and favoured round eye glasses without rims. Rose had been resolutely neat and decidedly old-fashioned; her grandson was an up-to-date go-getter if a bit of a slob. In fact, Castle thought, he could more easily picture the kid as being Detective Koronicki's grandson.

"Come in, come in. Glad to see you. I heard about you. Have a seat if you can find a place to sit. Trouble with living where you work. You want coffee?"

Jerry Fraser was a tall but small-boned kid who hadn't spent a minute outside taking in the Indian summer sun, or the regular summer sun either. Except for fingers stained by cigarettes and newsprint, the kid's skin was the colour of a cod fish's belly. His mousey hair looked pasted on in patches. He could have used a change of clothes and a good long bath.

Jerry ducked into the kitchen, popped out in a few seconds with two cups of coffee. "Keep a pot on all day, all night. Must drink twenty-thirty cups a day."

He fairly thrust a cup at Castle who figured the cup must be extremely hot but, no—Jerry had been seized by the need to give his head an energetic scratch. As he did so, Castle saw little white spots appear on Jerry's blue shirt, and instinctively put his hand over his cup.

"I don't sleep much. Insomniac. We don't need as much sleep as we think we do. Why spend a third of your life sleeping, eh?"

"Don't get much shut-eye myself," Castle said but it hardly mattered whether he made any reply, the kid just kept talking. Jerry had read something somewhere about how to train yourself to get by on less sleep; he mentioned taking a course that taught you how to read faster which was of the utmost importance in his work. Castle nodded every ten seconds and that seemed to satifsy the kid; meanwhile he looked around the room. Rose's old sofa, doilies gone, mounds of business books and papers on the cushions where suffragettes and old Wobblies used to sit. Rose's books—Johann Most, Rudolf Rocker, Max Stirner, Alexander Berkman, Jack London, all the rest of them, even Emily Murphy—gone, replaced by *Alberta Gold Mining Industry Annual Report*, *How to Win Friends and Influence People*, *The Ten Step Path to Financial Independence*, *International Investment Made Easy.* Rose's desk was there and her typewriter from the dawn of the mechanical era. There was also an efficient-looking Underwood and another typewriter at the end of the desk, a streamlined machine called an Aldon which put Castle in mind of the Adlon Hotel in Berlin that catered to Nazis and their friends.

"How come you have three typewriters?" Castle asked, mainly

to break the kid's monologue.

"One's for the Financial Report, the other for letters and such."

"What about Rose's?"

"Well, guess I keep it around out of nostalgia. Tried using it once but it was no go. Those keys have typed out so much anarchist folderol, they must have been rebelling."

"I'll let that one pass. So what exactly is in your paper?"

"Research that's what's in it. A wealth of research. Information to aid the investor. All day I work on the paper, and half the night. Now twenty-five cents may at first seem like a lot to spend but it isn't when you consider all those hours I put in looking things up, all those phone calls digging for leads and clues. And what's more last week's issue, last month's issue, is as good as new. That kind of information doesn't go out of date. The reader, the potential investor, doesn't have the time to dig out all the dope I provide him with. And he probably couldn't get it anyway. Here I'll show you. I'll get some copies and stuff from the other room."

"Okay, while you're in there, I'll use the washroom," Castle said.

The bathtub was filled with more books and papers and binders, and Castle reckoned it allowed the kid some excuse for not keeping up with his personal hygiene. As he stood over the toilet bowl, Castle studied the familiar poster of his old buddy Pierre Joseph Proudhon, bucolic hills and fields in back of him, and above him, the legend, "Property is Theft." When Castle came out, he found Jerry standing in the middle of the livingroom, shifting his weight from one foot to the other, holding Rose's thick scrapbook and copies of the Financial Report.

"So here're some copies, see for yourself." He dumped them in Castle's arms. "You noticed the poster in there, eh? Property is theft. I think that's pretty funny. And ironic, I mean, me having it on the wall after she had it. My grandmother's notions, I think, personally, were always unrealistic. Downright silly in her day but even sillier now. Property is theft! Come on, now. The guy must have been off his rocker to come up with that."

"Jerry, I don't want to stand in your living room and debate anarchist philosophy with you, especially not with the world going to hell in a handcart the way it is but I should hope that you, being a guy who, as you've indicated, looks below the surface of things, should spare a minute or two for that old boy Proudhon."

"Why," Jerry grinned, "waste a minute or two?"

"Because you'd find that he wasn't off his rocker even if Rudolf was."

"What's that?"

"Never mind. And neither was your grandmother. Off her rocker, I mean. You'd lose your irony but maybe gain an ally where you least expected it. Proudhon meant property in the sense of usurping land to enslave people. Proudhon himself was all for owning land because it protects you from the state."

Jerry stared at him blankly before saying, "No kidding?"

"No kidding."

He nodded his head, said, "I'll have to look into that."

And for just the briefest moment, Jerry Jenkins reminded Castle of grandmother Rose. The expression of open inquistiveness. But it was gone as he added, "Now I'd like to stand here and chat with you some more about grandmother Rose and her interests but time is money, isn't it? And I don't think it was Proudhon who said that."

"He sure didn't but it sure is. And since that's the case, get your meter running, kid. I want the lowdown on a certain company."

"Okay, ask me anything about anybody. If I can't refer you to a back issue or answer off the top of my head, I'll work up a report, get it to you right away. Like I say, I don't sleep at night, at least not very much, and I know most of the companies and...."

"Byerstock Investments."

"Uh...Byer..." The kid skidded to a halt between two consonants.

"What's up? Never heard of them?"

"I've heard of them. Yes, I have."

"Something the matter?"

The kid gave his head a scratch.

"They're involved in mining properties, real estate. Export Canadian craft goods to Europe, import scientific instruments and equipment."

"What do you mean Canadian craft goods? Like Cowichan sweaters, phoney indian masks? That sort of thing?"

"That's it. And any kind of wild west stuff."

"What kind of scientific instruments and equipment?"

"Any kind. Fine stuff, I hear. Laboratory equipment, lenses, medical tools, general all-around research material. I mean, I guess that's what it is. They do real well."

"What countries in Europe they deal with? Germany?"

"Sure. Or at least they had been dealing with Germany. I mean, you want fine craftsmanship, you get it from Germany right? You have cowboy and indian stuff and you send it to Europe, you don't send it to the Portuguese. It's the Germans who're crazy for all that, right? But since we're at war, they had to stop that."

"Has stock gone down at all since war was declared? Is it at the same level? What?"

"Hold on. I'll tell you in a second."

There were sheets of paper pinned to the wall above a shelf in back of his typewriter table. Jerry told Castle that he kept the last seven days worth of stock market quotations on the wall, and the last year's, stacked week by week, on the shelf. Other years were filed in boxes.

"Stock's actually gone up a point and a half in the few weeks since we declared war."

"What about the people involved? This Gus Tod, for instance?"

Castle felt slightly foolish standing in the middle of the cluttered apartment, arms extended, holding Financial Reports and Rose's twelve pound scrapbook.

"Well Gus Tod I know only by reputation."

"Is it a good reputation?"

"It's a mysterious reputation. You might call him a shadowy figure. You go by their office there at Howe and Helmecken and you won't run into him. I don't actually know of anybody who has run into him."

"I go by there who am I liable to run into?"

"A secretary. It is sort of unexpected, a successful outfit like they are and they have a tiny office and the girl answering the phone is the only person there. There's another guy who's supposed to be in charge of day-to-day operation, but you go around there, you wouldn't find him either. Name of Redman."

"Okay, thanks Jerry. My—" Castle was just about to tell the kid his address so he could send him a bill when the name registered, "You said Redman?"

"Yeah, Sherman Redman. Look, I'm going to say this because you were a friend of my Grandmother's...."

"A good friend."

"Yeah. Well, I have to do business with these people, with business people, and it would be bad for me if it got around I was talking out of class."

"It won't. Get around, that is."

"It's not even as if I have something concrete to say about this man. Anything particular he's done."

"You mean, Sherman Redman?"

"Yeah. Let me just put it this way, you hear rumours."

"Suppose I was a fellow who had some associates with a bit of money to invest and I came here to prevail upon your expertise, obtain a little discrete financial counselling. Suppose I told you my compatriots were thinking of putting some money into Byerstock Investments on account of it appears to be an up and coming outfit. What would you tell me?—knowing I would pass along the results of your counseling without, of course, mentioning your name."

"I'd say if you or the parties to whom you intend to convey anything gleaned from my counseling were considering investing a little bit of dough for a short period of time and didn't care what this particular company might be involved in—and I stress, might be—well, I'd tell you, go right ahead. But if a company is involved in areas that are not exactly tasteful or ethical, odds are that it may get its comeuppance. A fact which makes long term involvement or heavy investment appear not so promising."

"So the people behind this particular company are not folks dear old Rose would look favourably upon?"

"Hell, my Grandmother wouldn't look favourably upon ninety-nine-and-a-half percent of the people I deal with. Them being dastardly capitalists, you understand. But these particular capitalists... well, my dear old Grandmother was an anarchist, and if I understand it right, anarchists ain't all pacifists."

"You heard right. Send me a bill."

"Forget it."

Chapter Seven

The Canadian National Railway station always reminded Castle of an Edwardian frog squatting there on Main Street ready to make the leap to False Creek. Inside there was a vast hallway, plenty of cement and marble, and several plaster curlicues that the ladies of the Ladies' Civic Arts Club on their cultural tours were given to calling "cartouches," pronouncing the word so the last syllable sounded like cute rear ends in yiddish.

There were murals too, painted to glorify the workers who pushed the railroad through forests, over prairies and mountains and made this sprawling country whole. Nation builders they were, as well as navvies. Most of the actual navvies were not heroic looking white fellows like those in the paintings—hell, those guys looked like tall versions of Joe Frontenac —no, they were Chinese coolies but, well, never mind.

Castle and Louise Jones were striding across the polished floor, past the cement pillars and the heroic murals and the cartouches that you expected to present some devastating universal and timeless pronouncement from Seneca or Marcus Aurelius—maybe about property—but instead spelled out the names of the Scottish mutton chops who bankrolled the project. Castle and Louise crossed the hall and went out the backdoors and there were the trains in the smoke. Castle loved that smell. There was nothing like it, the smell of burning iron, the air full of soot. One problem was: he wasn't going; the other problem: Louise was.

She had her ticket and they had five minutes.

Other members of the troupe were on the platform too but they barely acknowledged each other, if at all, respectful of farewells.

"Always gives me a little thrill," Louise said.

"Yeah, me too. You and I, kid, we were born to wander. Most others need to stay in one place and collect all the paraphenalia of daily living but not us. We're throwbacks to what the species is supposed to be: nomads. Why..."

"Gees, you sound like Joe Frontenac."

"Sorry."

"Nevertheless, even though I'm only going to Coutts, Alberta. I still get a little thrill."

"Hey, you're about to depart on a big adventure. Think of all those boys ready to be shipped Over There, and they're scared though they'd never admit it. They're half hoping the fighting starts for real and half wishing they were back safe in a relief camp. They know the big bad Boche is waiting for them. And you, Louise Jones, are there to give them a fond little memory to carry as they jump from tree to tree. The memory of your smile, the way you shuffled off to Buffalo."

"My rear end."

"What?"

"That's what they'll recall. Or the way I'm supposed to flip up my skirt in back after I leave the doctor's office in that one skit."

"Well that too, of course."

"Aren't you jealous?"

"Sure I am, doll. No Canuck doughboy over in France or Italy or Beligum or someplace better have a memory of your rear end or any other part of you. That's all I got to say about it."

"It's sad, Gene. Thinking about them going over to, well, to die. It's going to get bad isn't it?"

"Yeah, I think it's going to get real bad."

"This base we're going to for the first shows? Coutts, Alberta? It's right on the borderline."

"Yeah, I was there with the carnival, weren't you?"

"No, never. Anyway, what I heard, in the week between Great Britain declaring war and us declaring war although everyone knew we were going to, the Americans stood on their side of the line and we on ours, and we tossed them ropes and they tied them around the fighter planes, and we pulled them across the border. Because we weren't prepared."

"Still aren't."

"Well here's the fellow shouting 'All aboard.' I wish we were both aboarding. On the Orient Express or something. Couldn't you find some private eye work where you have to take the Orient Express?"

"Come to think of it, I know a young lady once, was a grandaughter of old Nagelmackers."

"Hell does that mean?"

"Means I might have an in. Or, I had an in, so to speak."

"I'm not sure you know what you're talking about."

Unfortunately, they were standing right by Louise's car so they couldn't fill the last awkward seconds by walking hurriedly. Fortunately, a negro man filled the last seconds for them. He was in a starched uniform and razor-creased black slacks, a porter.

"Sorry, folks. Time to go. Oh, excuse me, sir. Are you Gene Castle?"

"Yeah, I am. And you?"

"Sam Case. I was talking to Raymond Thomas yesterday morning right before you came over to the short. Good morning, ma'am. I know your name too, Miss Jones."

"Glad to meet you, Sam."

"I play over at the Retreat. A little trumpet. I know Raymond's hoping you'll come by soon. And Miss Jones, too. Pardon me for interrupting but since we got to be pulling out..."

"I'll see you there, Sam. But Louise's is going to be away. Do me a favour, eh? If she talks to too many men, let me know."

"Oh, yes sir. Yes sir."

Castle caught Case's ironic glance after that last 'Yes sir' and gave him the slightest of nods. Case returned the slightest of smiles. The conductor broke it up, shooing everybody aboard, touching elbows so no one would take a tumble off the wooden portable step.

And then Castle was on the platform with the other loved ones, the loved and the left. There was a hiss of steam, more smoke and the big train pulled away, people leaning out the windows waving.

Castle thinking, I don't see her for over a year, then I see her a few days and we separate again. Fourteen years since I met her and we've been apart most of that time. Hell, that makes us practically newlyweds. Or we would be if we were married. She'd never mentioned it; neither had he.

Castle walked away but he didn't have to walk far. Larry Sobell was waiting for him in a booth in the train station restaurant. The fat man saw Castle, glanced at his watch, the one with the frayed band. "You're right on time."

"Train was on time."

"Maybe Mussolini came over fixed all that."

"Started out as a socialist, old Benito."

"You say that as if you know him."

"Almost. Met some of his close cronies."

"So some day maybe you can tell me. But first, are you, at heart, a counter guy or a booth guy?"

"At heart, Larry, I'm a counter guy even though the place I go to in the morning I got to sit in a booth. There're guys been going into the joint a few decades longer than me and they have priority. One of them dies, a stool becomes vacant."

"Sort of like the French Academy."

"Yeah. How about you?"

"I'm a counter guy but force of circumstance turned me into a booth guy. I got too fat for the stools."

A young man barely out of his teens took Castle's order for French toast. Sobell said, "I like old waitresses too. Not kids. I got a lot of likes and dislikes. Breakfast I want kasha and eggs, a nice bialy. Think I can get that?"

"Sure it's right there on the board with the breakfast specials over there next to that contraption with the flaps with advertisements on them. One flap flips over every thirty seconds on account of most of us are slow readers. See it? You can also get matzoh balls, gefilte fish."

Sobell grinned, murmured 'gefilte fish' as if to himself and out loud, said, "So did you find out who's behind the obituaries?"

"Yeah, I did."

Sobell nodded. "You're pretty good at this."

"Luck helps. You know Sherman Redman?"

Sobell had been about to bite a piece of toast with undulating hills of strawberry jam. He stopped, put the toast down on the plate. Sobell seemed to be digesting what he'd just heard. He shook his head slowly, muttered, "Why me?"

"What'd you mean, why me?"

"Never mind, I know why me."

"You know this Redman?"

Sobell didn't say anything.

"The way I understand it he's not going to be the Chamber of Commerce's outstanding business ambassador of the year."

"This is a man I don't think I want to discuss."

"Larry, excuse me for mentioning it but you look awfully uncomfortable at the mention of this fellow."

"I never met him."

"Then why would he send you obituary notices?"

"Here..." Sobell handed Castle an envelope. "There's a hundred dollars inside."

"Thanks but wait a minute..."

Sobell shook his head, got up, "I'll get the cheque. You did the job I asked you to do. I like you. Maybe we'll run into each other sometime. See you."

Castle watched him go. Sobell was wearing a different seersucker suit. This one had pale green instead of pale blue stripes. He had the fat man's side-to-side gait. Why did he dismiss me so abruptly, Castle wondered. Just when we were getting along so well. A couple of frustrated counter guys.

Instead of crossing the big lobby again and seeing the murals and the cartouches, Castle took the side entrance. It had started to drizzle. Around here were trainyards and factories, dirty brick warehouses with rusting iron freight doors and loading ramps that trucks had backed into thousands of times. Before he'd left town, in the deepest Depression, those ramps were filled, of an evening, with the prone, tattered forms of men, and more than a few women, who had no place else to go. These were new times but either way you looked, up or down the Avenue, it was the same: it was bleak. He hated the name of it. Terminal Avenue.

But hell he had a brand new hundred dollar bill in his pocket and it was only eight o'clock of a brand new morning. Best to look at it that way, Castle told himself.

But another way of looking at it is: I do have that hundred dollar bill but only about fourteen other bills, all of them singles. I'm forty-three years old. My woman's gone for I don't know how long. I've just come back from three years having had any traces of hope for a better world smashed. My country has gone to war. And I'm an old carney walking in the rain with a knife in my sock garter. I better turn off Terminal Avenue right here, right quick.

He killed two hours drinking coffee in three different joints, read the papers, and when he thought Joe Frontenac might be in the office, went over to the Times Building. The receptionist let him pass through to the inner sanctum of the editorial department. He still brought with him a whiff of adventure. He could tell it from the expressions of the workers. He could also tell it was a fading glory based on old exploits. Castle liked the look of the editorial department, the sound and even the smell of it. Like coffee and typewriter ribbons and eraser crumbs. People banging away on machines, phones ringing, shouts and answers. Couple of youngsters dashing across the floor with yellow sheets of paper in their hands. The Poo Bahs at the horseshoe with dealer's shades.

There was Joe Frontenac at the back. He had more space around his desk than the other people. He was by way of being the star. Joe was reading from foolscap and grinning to himself.

"Admiring your own copy, are you?"

"Thanks for introducing me to Matty Muldoon. Spent about five hours with him. Could hardly tear myself away. Didn't want to. What a guy. I took your advice too and did the 'He was there' thing. 'Matty Muldoon, he was there. He was there in the days of sail. There in '81, when there wasn't even a Vancouver, but up the coast, the Nootka had half a dozen English hostages and Matty Muldoon in a bum boat with four other guys went ashore in the dead of night and rescued those six wretched Caucasians...He was there. Matty Muldoon was there in Valparaiso in '07, caught in the middle of a revolution when the whole damn harbour blew.... He was there'....

etcetera, etcetera... and then I close by saying, 'He was always there. He will always be there. Matty Muldoon. The eternal sailor.'"

Frontenac leaned back and beamed. The guy sure likes himself, Castle thought. Hell, I like him too. He's as obvious as a tow-headed tyke waking up on Christmas morning.

"What do you think?"

"I don't know, Joe. It might need a little work."

"What do you mean! Oh, you're only kidding me, aren't you?"

"Yeah, yeah. Your style is—what you call it?—sacrosanct. Now, as you know, you owe me a favour. The guy I mentioned the other day. Asked you if you ever heard of him?"

"Redman."

"That's right. I sure admire your reporter's memory. Anyway, if you can dig up anything on him in the morgue or elsewhere I'd appreciate it. Also anything on a guy named Gus Tod."

"When do you want it?"

"You can give it to me late tomorrow night at an afterhours shebeen called The Porter's Retreat on Homer Street. I'm going there for a meet with a guy and we can hear a singer that's supposed to be a combination Billie Holiday and Lee Wiley."

"Sure, she is. And I'm a combination Richard Harding Davis and Clark Gable."

"Ah, I see through you, Frontenac. You're just waiting for me to say something like, 'But you are.'"

The ace reporter blushed.

CHAPTER EIGHT

If you were Madame Hanska peeking through beaded curtains covering the bottom floor front window of your fortune teller's shop on Homer Street, you'd probably be sorely irked because of all the folks you saw going up the walkway between two wooden buildings across the way, turning left halfway along, knocking on the door and being let in. Most of them being let in anyway. If Madame Hanska was peeking after midnight, she could count at least one person every few minutes or so going in there. Most of them were coloureds but there was a white person every now and again. She certainly never turned anyone away but, then again, an entire night might go by without a single soul knocking on her door. Chinese, coloured, or lily white. Palm reading, tea leaves, crystal ball gazing. She did the whole bit. Even arrange a seance, commune with your dead Auntie Fannie, you wanted. Madame Hanska billed herself as a "Genuine Gypsy Sorceress." Hell, she was just a black Irish bint from Montreal and hers your standard carney flat store-mitt camp gaff but who's to know? Certainly not all those coloureds. Madame Hanska had half a mind to go over there, see what exactly was drawing the crowds. It wasn't just the jungle music. No it was that frail she'd heard the talk about. She was itching to see the girl close up but she wouldn't want the girl to see her in case the girl really was a gypsy. It wouldn't do to be exposed for the gadja she was. Now there're two white fellows going up between the houses right now. Madame Hanska felt like running over, holding up her voluminous skirts, boot heels clicking, hoop earrings jangling, grabbing them, "Hey, white boys. Come with me, I will tell you what lies in store."

Castle and Frontenac entered in the middle of the tenor's solo on 'Moonbeam.' The guy at the door couldn't have been more than six feet-five and probably didn't weigh an ounce over 260 pounds. He looked at Castle curiously but after Castle mentioned Raymond Thomas' name, the wide man let them pass in.

The club was dark and high-ceilinged and took up most of an entire floor in the big wooden house. Half the joint was below ground and the blacked out windows were above your head. There were a couple of weak lights at either end of the bar, a light over the stage, candles on the tables. They walked to an empty table in the back. Frontenac sat down, nodded his head toward the door man. "That guy, see the way he looked at us? Like he thought we were Captain and First Mate on the original slave ship."

"Yeah, I got a feeling folks don't shuck down in here."

Frontenac was in a mood to elaborate but Castle turned his attention to the stage and this discouraged the reporter. The tenor, a gangly man wearing sunglasses, finished his solo and turned it over to the trumpet. It took a few bars for Castle to realize the player was Sam Case, the porter he'd met at the train station with Louise. The musicians traded off, going around—piano, sax, trumpet, bass, drums—then coming together to finish up. Only when they were done the tune did a waitress appear to take their order.

They watched her return to the bar; black skirt, starched white blouse. She was big and curvy, and Frontenac was commenting on the fact that some women could put on the pounds and keep the curves while others just got wide all over, and wasn't that a curious thing, when another man appeared on stage, stepped to the microphone stand.

"Ladies and gentlemen. So glad to see you here at The Porters' Retreat, a refuge for the brethren—and some select friends—a retreat from the vicissitudes of life on the other side of the door."

This garnered a round of applause, some whistles.

"Okay. Now I know another reason why you all are here. And we're going to bring her out in a moment."

More applause.

"I am here to tell you good people that you are not about to see anything like her if you climb to the top of any downtown hotel, visit any old Palomar or Panorama Room. Yes indeed and yes sirree. This young lady is not only from the other side of the door, she comes to us from the other side of the world. Straight from the caravans of the Carpathians...."

The drummer served up a rim shot, and Castle leaned over the table, spoke in back of his hand to Frontenac. "'Caravans of the Carpathians.' Maybe you can use that, Joe."

"She is indeed a gypsy woman. Learned to sing around the campfires with her people and the great Django Reinhardt. Let's here it for her. Galatea Monti...Put your hands together!"

The woman didn't walk out so much as she seemed to glide, like under that floor length-clinging black dress there were wheels on her shoes, little silver angel wheels, and the emcee was pulling her by invisible strings from the other side of the stage. Her hair was as black as you'd figure but not cascading in waves to the shoulders like the cliche of a sultry gitana. It was in bangs across her forehead, cut to just over the eyebrows, and in back fell to about the middle of her neck. She started to sing, "What is this Thing Called Love?"

After she'd done the first two verses—standing absolutely still, phrasing in a sleepy almost deadpan manner—the group entered and Castle gave a start when Joe Frontenac spoke, "I don't know what this thing called love is but I think I just fell in it."

Castle realized he had been lost, caught up in the song. As Frontenac extolled the woman's charms, Castle tried to explain it to himself, settling on: She's just so different, it's totally unexpected.

He was almost convinced there was nothing more to it than that, when Galatea Monti stepped to the microphone again.

"Jesus, Castle. What a dame. She's electric. I can practically feel it in the air."

"Sure, Joe but do me a favour, eh? Whisper like I'm doing." Castle glanced over at the next table. "I want to hear the music and also if you keep talking so loud that guy over there might decide to decorate one of your cheeks with a razor scar like the one he's got."

"Yeah, yeah." Frontenac whispered, "But the dame is causing the entire goddamn magnetic field to be rearranged. You mean you didn't notice? Tell me I'm not completely crazy.

"Okay, maybe you're not completely crazy."

When the number finished, Castle looked around again, said to Frontenac: "I never seen so many Negroes clapping for a white person before."

He also noticed people looking at each other as if to say, 'You hear what I just heard?'

"What in hell are gyspies anyway?" Frontenac asked. "From India? Persian outcasts? A lost tribe of Israel?"

"I wonder if she's really one of the rom. Hard to tell what she is from way back here."

"Yeah. But I'm afraid to get any closer."

"Come on, Joe. Don't overdo it.'

Galatea Monti, as if aware of the effect she'd had on at least one member of the audience, introduced her next number like she wanted to rub it in, her speaking voice low and sounding satisified, like she'd sampled certain pleasures, had enough of a rest now and was ready to try them again.

"This is Cab Calloway tune which Marlene Dietrich she was singing in a movie some time ago called, 'Crazy Voodoo.'"

Castle remembered that one. *Blonde Venus*, it was called. Dietrich coming out in a gorilla costume to the beating of drums. You don't know it's her, of course. She takes off the suit, bit by bit, slowly, first you see her forearm and long elegant fingers. When she does the number her manner and the lyrics are just so incongruous, and more effective for that. This woman had much of that style only she was a better singer. An authentic jazz singer. She put the lyrics over with a sort of erotic lassitude.

She did half a dozen more numbers, ending the set with something called, "A Girl Who Likes to Mingle," that had many in the crowd talking back to her but, Castle noted, in an understated way. Someone else singing those words, they would have been raucous.

I'm a girl who likes to mingle
soft lights and scintillating
conversation that's what I like
especially late at night
It gives me such a tingle

And she ended the verse with :

All over....

There was plenty of oohing and aahing then, and she left them that way. A simple nod and Galatea Monti slipped off stage. She did not come back out for an encore despite the enthusiastic applause.

The clapping had barely subsided when Raymond Thomas appeared at the table, "Well, Gene, what do you think of our new chanteuse?"

"Hey there, Raymond. Yeah, pretty good."

"Absolutely first rate." Frontenac said. "What a dame. Sends shivers down my spine."

Raymond Thomas looked down at the reporter with a slightly bemused expression. After Castle introduced them, Thomas said, "Well then if you think she's so special, and she is—a really unique talent—you might want to come back now and meet her. After that we can talk, eh Gene?"

"Sure, Raymond. And Joe did a little digging into that same matter which we discussed although he has not yet hipped me as to what he came up with."

Thomas regarded Frontenac again, as if appraising him, said, "Of course."

The two men got up and followed Thomas through the crowd and around the side of the stage. Thomas knocked on a door at the end of twenty feet of hallway. The woman answering, "Who is it?"—saying the 'is' like 'ease,' the last word coming out, 'et?'

"It's Raymond. With a couple of friends."

"Very well. Come in."

Thomas, hand on the doorknob, whispering to them, "She don't usually let people in here."

"You're a lucky man," Frontenac whispered back.

It was a tiny room and Galatea Monti was seated on a piano bench in front of a small wooden table dominated by a make-up mirror framed by light bulbs. When Thomas started with the introductions, she turned away from the mirror, and Castle said, "Please don't get up, Miss Monti."

She looked at him then directly. Big eyes, a curious dark grey. Castle suddenly and for the briefest moment felt like he had lost his balance. The woman quickly turned her gaze to Frontenac who was full of praise for her performance. Castle didn't want to look at her, looked around the room instead. She had to share her bench and table with wooden crates, some two-by-fours leaning in a corner, and a ladderback chair occupied by a paint can. The table held relatively few make up items, some lipstick tubes, a round powder box, other things. There was a pitch pipe too and it seemed to fit right in with the other stuff. There was also a small photo stuck into the frame of the make-up mirror. A very respectable looking guy in a suit, maybe it was a picture of her father.

Frontenac was still prosing, the woman regarding him without any expression whatsoever. Then she crossed her legs, it sounded like silk being slowly ripped. Castle looked toward the sound, and she looked at him and this time there was a hint of something in her face that was almost surprise. And then they both glanced at Frontenac. Castle noticing the reporter trying to stand straight and tall. Galatea Monti finally spoke, saying to Joe, "You are too kind. Now if you will permit me..."

Frontenac looked about to say something else but Castle gave the reporter's elbow a tug.

A couple of minutes later, the three men were back at the table. Castle seeing a fresh drink at his place, thinking it more than a bit curious that he didn't remember the trip, at least step by step, from the dressing room.

"Yeah, that's a special dame," Frontenac was saying. "In fact, she must be the most beautiful woman I've ever seen."

"Come on, Joe," Castle put in. " You're always saying that. Remember the English woman who worked at Garmano's place on Union Street? And then there was the young girl in Spain. Where was it, Avila? We were passing through town and she was with some other girls near the fountain. The older women were doing the washing and the girls were there sharing a mirror and one of them looked from the mirror to us. And you turned to me, 'She's must be the most...' etcetera."

"This time I mean it. Look, you know that picture they're showing at the Strand? Hotel for Women? The dames in that, Ann Sothern,

Linda Darnell, they're a couple of head turners, no question about it. Even better, Ecstasy. It's at the Dominion. They named that one right. That Hedy Lamarr, she'd put lead in a dead man's pencil. Last weekend our competition runs a photo of Greta Garbo in their magazine and inside they had a short story by one of your favourties, Gene. I mean Thyra Samler Winslow. And it was called The Best Looking Girl in Town. Well, what I want to say, you put all those frails in a town where you got Galatea Monti, well, the rest of them are going to have to go to some other town where they can fight for that title."

"Thyra Samler Winslow?" Castle said.

Raymond Thomas had done nothing, either by comment or gesture to indicate he had any opinion whatsoever about the woman. "That's all well and good but suppose we get down to business."

"Byerstock Investments," Castle said. "Well capitalized. They have gold mining properties, some real estate holdings. Export craft items to Europe, mainly to Germany. Import scientific material although what exactly that includes, I'm not sure. Also mostly from Germany. Head of the company is an elusive gent named Gus Tod but the fellow I heard runs the show is a character called Sherman Redman."

"That last is fact? Not that it matters."

"Never know, it might," Frontenac interjected. Thomas regarded him, turned back to Castle.

"Evidently it's the McCoy. You want hearsay? I have fairly reliable hearsay as well as investment advice from someone who doesn't want to be named but is in a position to know."

"Give me the fairly reliable first."

"Which is that Sherman Redman runs an insurance fraud operation. Has guys steal stuff for his buddies, shares in the money they collect, as well as the proceeds from fencing the items."

"How fairly reliable is that information?"

"Comes from the guy who perpetrates the robberies and runs errands for Redmond."

What kind of errands?"

"One thing is Sherman gets a kick out of sending obituaries to at least one fellow he hardly knows. Don't ask me why."

Raymond Thomas nodded, asked Castle, "And what investment advice did you receive?"

"Fellow is of the opinion that a brief and fleeting affair with Byerstock Investments is the most a punter should risk. But a wise man with serious money to spend who's looking for something'll last, should go elsewhere. Or, to quote exactly, 'I'd run the other way if I saw anyone who had anything to do with Byerstock.'"

"Yeah," Frontenac said, "But the trouble is, nobody knows what anybody who has anything to do with Byerstock looks like."

"Well I believe," Raymond Thomas said. "This is one outfit that Guy and I will stay well clear of. What do I owe you, Gene?"

"Not a damn thing unless you want to give me a ride in your new Cadillac automobile sometimes."

"It's a deal. I'll wear the cap too."

"Good. I wouldn't have it any other way."

"I'll even stand you all to another drink."

"Not for me," Castle said. "I have to get going."

"Well I'm sticking around," Frontenac said. "I didn't see nearly enough of Miss Galatea Monti. How could anyone see enough of her?"

"Better cool your motor, gates," said Thomas. "Young lady's got a husband."

"I knew there had to be a catch."

Castle said his goodbyes as the lights dimmed, the spot hit the centre of the stage and Galatea Monti came toward it.

Ten minutes later, two in the morning, Castle was walking down Cordova Street and glimpsed up ahead the sign for the Rose Hotel. When he was at the entrance to the place he took a close look at the sign, thought about all the other times he'd looked at it, seeing but not seeing it. Then he went up to the room, and pulled a chair over to the window, poured himself a shot of dark rum, and looked at the sign from another angle. He looked and drank, and long about three o'clock, an automobile passed by down on the street and the glow from its headlights came in the window bringing the shadow of the hotel sign with it and together they travelled across the ceiling, down a wall and over the double bed before vanishing.

CHAPTER NINE

Two jobs the first day but over the next week Castle hardly did anything at all. He was like the rookie who busted out on opening day, slashing line drives all over the outfield but then the hurlers got his number, held him to a Texas League single the rest of the week, and the manager set him down on the bench.

He worked just an hour and a half, escorting a rich and tough old socialist named Harlan Dewey, and his daughter, from his house to the bank. The rich and tough old socialist kept his money in his mattress in his mansion out near Stanley Park. Didn't believe in banks. But Dewey was in his middle-eighties and the daughter who was in her middle-fifties convinced him he should trust the money to dependable old Bank of Montreal. It was for his own good, don't you know. Hoodlums might hear he had money in his mattress, come in and knock him over the head, take it away. The old man smoked those big long cigars and Castle could almost read the daughter's mind, thinking about him lying back in bed puffing away, reading his Upton Sinclair novels for the umpteenth time, falling asleep and burning the place down. The mattress would go first. The woman kept her eye on the suitcase and the guy holding it all the way from Denman and Comox to the bank. Didn't even give dear old cane-wielding dad a glance. Castle was the guy holding it. After the deposit was made, she'd turned to Castle, dismissing him, "Send Dad the bill."

Dewey saying, "That's not the agreement. He gets paid now."

"But Dad."

"Give him the goddamned money."

She started to protest and Castle saw the guys knuckles tighten on the crook of his cane. Tight and hard, hardly any skin on them, fierce. Like he wanted to use them to hit somebody, like in the old days, some scab or strawboss. And he was sorry as hell he wasn't able. The old man's eyes reminded Castle of his knuckles. The daughter grudgingly took the bills out of her bag, a couple of tens, holding them with the tip of her thumb and index finger. Other fingers keeping out of the way. The old man patted Castle on the backside with the cane. "See you, Gene."

So you see Gene in his office now, feet propped up on the desk, sipping bookend rum and reading volume 15 of the encyclopedia, 'Maryb to Mushet.' He hadn't made much money in the past seven days but he knew all about Mfumbiro and Miaotsze. He'd read, drank rum and rye, walked the streets, run into Frank Evans who, having fallen off the wagon, was swinging a pick axe on a day labour gig; he'd gone to the movies twice but avoided Hedy Lamarr both times. Instead he saw Greer Garson, that big doll, in Mr. Chips, and Ronald Colman, in *The Light That Failed.* He liked Ronald Colman. The man always seemed so sad, like he had a deep hurt he'd never shake and could never talk about—a dame probably, what else?—and was just waiting for the day's shooting to end so he could go out to the pool and dive into a gin and tonic. Castle pictured Frank Evans as Colman's pool boy. What a disaster that would be. Them getting loaded and taking tumbles off the deep end.

One thing Castle hadn't done during his perambulating days and loose-end nights was fall by the Porters' Retreat.

But then the Manager, some big galoot in the sky with a lump of Mail Pouch in his cheek and wearing the visiting team uniform, noticed Castle down at the end of the bench reading his encyclopedia, pointed a gnarled finger at him and jerked a fat thumb at the playing field. Castle sighed and put down Volume 15, he had just been moving in on Moloch. He got up, grabbed his club, headed for the on deck circle, and thought he noticed the Manager smiling slyly—as if over some joke only he knew about. And then the big galoot let fly a brown stream of juice toward the playing field.

Castle walked up the five wide steps to the Standard Building, carrying two cardboard cups of coffee, nudged the bottom of the revolving door with a toe, and crossed the marble lobby to Laura's dutch-door enclosure. She pulled out a wire, reached for the coffee and barely muttered thanks.

"Rough night?"

"Oh, yeah. Sure was. I drank a lot of hot cocoa and sat in front of the Motorola listening to Fred Allen and then the Happy Gang. But I never cracked a smile."

"Must be some continental gent's the cause."

"Him I see when he wants which isn't very often. He sends a car around. Oh, well. As for you, you got a message to please come around and see Manny Israel. It's important, and I'm quoting. That and you have business."

"Good. I need a break."

"This looks like trouble."

"That's my middle name."

"Double trouble. There's two of them."

"I got my blade. You think it's enough?"

"For the gent, maybe. A negro gent, he is. As for the doxie, a guy might need an entire army. She's got a hairdo reminds me of a helmet. It would look ridiculous on anyone else but on her it works. I don't like to admit it but yeah."

"Laura. Tell me. You being such an insightful individual. The woman and the negro gent. You think there's anything between them?"

Laura shrugged, blew at her coffee.

"They're both so smooth, it's hard to tell but I don't think so. The guy, well, he's a big, good-looking man even if he is a negro but he doesn't give off anything. I mean, a girl doesn't have to have eyes for the guy in question to notice such a thing. Am I right?"

"Sure, kid."

"As for the dame, well, what she gives off, and don't take this the wrong way, I'm not peculiar, what she gives off you could cut slices of and sell on the back streets of Paris. Front streets too. But, the negro gent? I don't think he's buying any of it."

"Thanks for the analysis."

"Yeah, you ever make any money you can put me on the payroll."

"I hope your big butter and egg man comes around soon."

"Yeah, me too. Gene, I got some advice for you. You go up those stairs, you sit at the desk, you have to look at that dame. But the whole time, you think about something else."

"Think about what?"

"You think about Louise. All those years with Louise."

They made quite a picture down at the end of the hallway; Raymond Thomas leaning against a radiator, rotating his chaffeur's cap in his big hands; Galatea Monti standing a few feet from him, standing perfectly still. The dirty window, rainstreaked behind them, smearing the view of the other building's eroded brown brick. They must have made an even stranger sight striding down the street. She had on a dark blue lightweight coat and a teal silk dress with matching heels. She was about five foot seven with legs as good as Dietrich's or Stanwyck's. Barbara Stanwyck never got enough credit for her legs. Yeah, the two of them must have turned some heads out there on the drizzly avenues.

"Hope you haven't been waiting long."

Thomas told him no, just five or so minutes. "You're a creature of habit, Gene. Usually come straight here from Ramona's."

He nodded to Galatea Monti, turned back to Raymond.

"Well, I'm trying to be like everyone else these days. Help the war effort by being reliable. Come on in."

Castle brought them inside, past the Chinese screens, pulled two chairs up to the desk. Raymond Thomas studied a picture on the wall. The woman sat in a chair.

"Why, that's Haile Selassie," Thomas said, in a kind of awed whisper. "That his signature at the bottom? Signed to you?"

"Yeah, the Lion and me, we were like this."

Thomas turned away from the wall.

"You are a man of mystery, Gene Castle. Hard to fathom."

"Well I hope so. You get in this private operative business, helps to be hard to fathom. Must be the same in your line of work.

Chaffeuring, I mean."

"That's right, got to smile and smile some more, and 'yassuh' all the greys meanwhile having your own thoughts that would be hard to fathom if anyone ever considered you were capable of having them."

Castle grinned and Thomas grinned. The woman stared at something on the desk. Castle assumed it was the tray with the pitchers and water glasses.

"You want a glass of water Mrs. Monti?"

"Miss Monti."

"I'm sorry, I thought..."

"I use my former name. Not that of my husband. No, I do not want a glass of water."

"You want a drink of something else? I have rum, rye."

She surprised him by accepting.

"Thank you. Rye. Um, neat."

She said 'neat' like it was a new word she had heard and was trying it out. Raymond Thomas didn't want anything. Castle not wanting her to drink alone at five after nine in the morning, poured himself a rye, pointed the glass at her but she just sipped. Oh, well, he thought, different customs.

"Okay," he said, looked at Raymond, looked at the woman.

"So, I don't use my husband's name which is being Redl. Heinrich Redl."

She took a deep breath, crossed her legs, glass in both hands on the top knee. Castle saw her do this, saw three or four inches of the inside of her thigh, the bottom leg, the stockings just beginning to darken. If she decided she wanted to uncross her legs, the top one would naturally have to lift as she began the move, and Castle would naturally have to see the spot where the stocking tops ended, something of that patch of olive skin.

All that came to him in a split second after which he told himself, Well, I wasn't staring. Asked himself, How could one not have noticed the woman cross her legs?

Fortunately, she hadn't said anything in that split second. She probably was not allowing him a nice long look, she probably was gathering her thoughts.

"My husband, he is gone."

She said the one sentence. Castle waiting for the next one. It didn't seem to be forthcoming. He looked from her to Raymond Thomas. Galatea Monti fixed her eyes on Castle's. He looked into hers and his insides went on an elevator ride. "You'll have to tell me more," he said, not looking away.

"Why would he go, your husband?" Prompting her.

"He did not go alone."

"You mean, he had a friend, friends, another..."

"Certainly that is not what I mean."

"Well, excuse me." Castle aware of being abrupt, aware of trying to hide the fact that the woman had him off his balance.

"Miss Monti, you've come here for my help. You are going to have to speak freely with me if you wish to receive that help. I realize it must be difficult. It is also, however, the only way I can be of assistance."

"He was taken away."

"Taken away by whom?"

She looked at her drink, still on her knee. Castle glanced where she looked, then a little lower, saw the inner thigh was exactly as it had been, and pushed back on his chair, trying to be casual about it. Letting the desk hide her legs. He glanced over his shoulder, out the window, and there in the shaft between two buildings was a drizzly swath of Burrard Inlet, boats working out there now in the grey water, same colour as the sky.

"They want him back in Germany. He is a Jew."

Castle nodded, encouraging her to go on but thinking—Don't they have enough Jews to kill without going after ones that got away? According to what you read in the papers, they weren't doing anything like that, the Germans. But anybody who'd been in Europe in the last five or six years and had eyes and ears had to know a little about such things. In Spain, the German officers captured by the Brigades or CNT, would brag about what was done to Jews in the Fatherland.

"Miss Monti, you'll have to tell me why they want him back in Germany."

"My husband is a scientist," she blurted this out and stopped.

Castle thinking, Oh no, another long pause. He looked at Thomas as if for assistance. But the woman exhaled wearily. "I will tell you everything. My husband, Heinrich Redl is a botanist and a chemist. Until last year, or one year and one half year ago perhaps it was, he was chief of some other scientists who—how do I say what they did? They took, for instance, plants from mostly jungles—Asia, South America—and somehow made from these plants, drugs for medicine. But since the year or so before we are leaving, the results of my husband's work has been put to other use. Very evil use. Poisons, chemical warfare it is called. For years we tried to get out of Germany. We had not a bad life but we understood very well that when my husband had completed his work, they would eliminate him. And me too."

"You're also Jewish?"

"No, but I am part rom. My father he was gypsy. From Slovenia. My mother part Russian from the Caucasus and part Irish. You know what is Slovenia?"

"Sure, it's a little old part of the Austro-Hapsburg empire up there nudging Italy. For this brief moment in time, part of Yugoslavia, yes? What area of Slovenia?"

"Istrian coast."

"You must not have done much singing around those romantic gypsy campfires, eh? Your father would have been ostracized for living with a gadja."

"Yes, but I did sing around the campfires you speak of. Just not those of my father's people. Later, when in Paris, I met first Josef Reinhardt and later Django, and I would go with them. They were happy there among the caravans more so than when in the city. The women would sing. I had been singing too. Learning to sing. I studied by listening to records. But the way the women made the verses, singing the words...how is that word?"

"The phrasing?"

"Yes, the phrasing. I was thinking, if only I could put that phrasing to jazz."

Her eyes were sparkling as she thought of it. Castle was watching those eyes sparkle. And there wasn't any husband there in those eyes, at least not during that moment. But then Raymond Thomas cleared his throat and shifted in his chair, and now the negro was there in the room and the husband was there too. Castle got a picture of Louise on stage someplace like Lethbridge or Drumheller. Louise entertaining the boys. Waking up with Louise in the Rose Hotel.

"Yes, well. After Kristalnacht we managed to get out. My husband Heinrich and myself. In Germany they do not like gypsies either. There are a few people—brave people—to help such as us. We reached France, we sailed from Le Havre for Montreal. We stayed in Montreal for six months, maybe more. My husband needed to rest. He was very sick. He is sick. Something with his lungs and heart. He is sick because of the experiments he conducted with plants. In Montreal at first was okay. But then it got very unpleasant. Some people in the government in Quebec, they are associated with people in France who do not like Jews, and they made it bad for Jews recently come from Germany. There are fascist organizations like Chalifoux Labour Club who said—say—their intention is to hang a socialist and a Jew from every lamppost. When that started, the Jewish community in Montreal no longer dared help us."

"What were you doing all this time to support yourself? Your husband worked?"

"No, he was not able. I was singing in the jazz clubs there. We had to live in the negro quarter. St. Antoine's it was called. There was okay. But to leave the quarter was not so good. I am singing then at Terminal Club and the Nemderoloc Club."

"The what?"

"Nemderoloc, the name."

Galatea Monti looked to Raymond Thomas. Raymond grinned at Castle, "Spell it backward."

Castle wrote it down on his blotter, smiled.

"You hep to it?" Raymond asked.

"I'm hep."

"Those clubs in Montreal," Raymond picking up the story, "they cater mostly to the people in the neighborhood, and the people in that neighborhood are mostly sleeping car porters and their families. When things became difficult for Miss Monti and Mr. Redl, they were advised by folks in St. Antoine to head for Vancouver. The main gentleman in the neighborhood, Little Tubby Sauser, convened a meeting at his headquarters on the top floor of Rufus Rockhead's hotel on Mountain Street. The outcome being to facilitate a train trip west as well as provide a few names and numbers."

"Also my husband had a friend here from Germany. A scientist, Herman Nussbaum. But we have never found him."

"And that," Raymond said, "is how come Miss Monti came to be singing at Porters' Retreat. Something she has been doing to much acclaim these last five weeks."

"Where have you been living and what has your husband been doing these same five weeks, Miss Monti?"

"We found an apartment on Princess Street. My husband has been trying to get his strength back. So he does not much activity. He walks to the park in the morning, sits there for an hour if the weather is good. He writes in his notebooks."

"What does he write? He keep a diary?"

"No, such a thing would never occur to him. The notebooks hold his formulas, formulae. Who was the first to use this plant for medicine or poison. He writes how it was used, how use has changed. I don't understand much more of it."

"What else you do together?"

"Two times we make excursion to Stanley Park but it tires Heinrich very much. Him, he used to trek through the jungle to search for plants. But he is still a scholar. He is with his books most of the time. When I have rehearsal in the afternoon, maybe he will come with me to Homer Street and sit at a table or sit in my dressing room. He likes very much the music. He has many times spoken to me of the music of the shetl, he hums the tunes. The feel of it I try also to put into my singing. You understand this?"

"Yeah, I think I do. When was the last time you saw him?"

"Yesterday afternoon. He was at the Porters' Retreat. I was rehearsing because there is a new piano player. Heinrich was at a table and between numbers he told me he was tired and wanted to go back to the apartment."

"So he left and you haven't seen him since?"

"Yes. That is right."

"And you had to sing last night?"

She nodded her head, "I am afraid I was not very good."

"That's not true, Galatea." Raymond said. "You were wonderful despite everything."

To Castle, Raymond said, "She must have put all her agony over her husband into her singing. It was really very moving."

Castle thinking Raymond sounded close to adulation. Then thinking that such a thing was maybe not so farfetched at all.

"Okay, you got home and he was gone?"

"Yes."

"Any indication that he had been at home? I mean, was there any sign that he had reached the apartment after leaving the club?"

"No, I saw no sign of this."

"But he could have been home and left again, eh? It's possible?"

"He smokes a pipe. He comes home from the club, makes tea, smokes a pipe, sits by the window and reads. The pipe, the tea, the books in the afternoon, they relax him. There were no fresh ashes. He had not made tea. There was not any sign that he had been home. I reached the apartment less than two hours after Heinrich left the club."

"How old is your husband?"

"He is forty-three years old next month."

The way she talked about him, Castle had pictured a guy fifty at the least, more like sixty.

"He have many friends in town?"

"No, he really knew no one. Only people he met at the club. Heinrich is not able to be such a man about town like he was in Germany before he got ill."

"You must know a lot of people though."

Castle aware of the way Raymond looked at him when he said that.

"I meet many people at the club."

"Do you see many of these people when you are not at the club?"

"No. When I leave the club I am exhausted. I want only to rest and be with my husband."

Castle didn't like the picture that was beginning to form in his mind. The one of her sashaying past the Birks Clock there at Granville and Georgia, heads spinning wildly, guys practically falling out in the street—and not only was she knock em down and drag em out gorgeous, Galatea Monti was immensely talented, intelligent and composed; in short, a woman who could have everything she wanted in the world not to mention just about any man she wanted, and she was singing in a tenderloin afterhours club and married to a guy who was sick and old before his time. Now if it wore Heinrich out to take a streetcar to Stanley Park and back, then it followed that the two of them weren't setting fire to the mattress up there in their Princess Street apartment, keeping the neighbours awake all night while they went through all the positions of the Ananga Ranga. Castle felt a little guilty for thinking all that but knew he'd be pretty damned stupid if he didn't think all that.

"Miss Monti, you said before that he was taken away. Who do you believe took him away?"

"Why agents of the Nazis, of course."

Yeah, of course, Castle said to himself. How stupid of me not to realize it. Couldn't be a lover, or a would-be lover.

"You must understand how valuable was my husband's work. What he did before with plants to make medicines, this work was applied to war activity."

"Aren't there other scientists capable of doing the same things?"

"Perhaps after many years someone would reach his level but that would be too late. My husband was not only a laboratory scientist but an explorer, as well, a plant explorer, so he had a thorough knowledge of what he was working with. Why he is sick, incurably sick, is because he tested his medicines on himself. After the rats, the guinea pigs, the rabbits, Heinrich took the medicine himself. He insisted that is what all pioneers in his field must do, have always done."

"So you want me to find these agents of the Nazis, as you call them."

"I want you to find my husband."

"All right. I will. Raymond, I need to go to the Retreat and look around."

"I'll open up for you now."

"No I want to be there this afternoon, same time of day as when Dr. Redl left the club yesterday. Miss Monti, I'll have to come to your apartment too and you'll have to be there. I want to come by after I go to the club."

"But what for?"

"I want to get a feeling for your husband, what he was like, where he spent most of his time. It may sound unusual perhaps but that's the way I work."

She didn't say yes, she didn't say no, she just looked at him with those big grey eyes.

"If you're worried, have a chaperone in attendance."

Castle aware as he spoke that it sounded defensive.

"As you wish."

Castle thinking he shouldn't have been defensive but he had every right to be irritated especially by her 'as you wish.' He was, afterall, trying to find her husband. Or, perhaps that wasn't her objective here; maybe making a show of looking for her husband was the objective.

He mentioned his fee. Castle always hated doing that. Maybe time and clients would help him get over it. He doubted it. Castle knew he could always count on Time, but as for the clients, when he pictured having enough of them, also in the picture was himself as a steady, reliable workaday fellow building up a business over the years; he saw the good guys winning the war and then there'd be a post-war boom and he would open up branches all through the west, and by the time he was able to mention the matter of his fee without embarrassment, he'd have reached the point where his hirelings did that sort of thing.

Clarence handed over a retainer without engendering any awkwardness, and the two of them got up to leave, Clarence saying, just making conversation, "When are you going to start on the case, Gene?"

"Right now."

"But you're not falling by the retreat until this afternoon, and not going to the apartment, you said, until after that. So where you going to start the work?"

"Same place I always do. The street."

They started for the door. Castle wanted to look elsewhere. He didn't want to watch the dame leave. Instead he looked at the sheets of paper on his desk. He always had a couple of sheets of paper on his desk. On these sheets of paper were written things like, "Now is the time for all good men to come to the aid of their party" or "Who's riding Stolen Kisses in the sixth on Saturday?" or "Ask Danny Klein the address of Harry Page from Halifax who bought it on the plains of Tereul. Send his wife a note."

They were props, the papers, but it wasn't sneaky, he told himself, they put the client at ease. Inspite of himself, he looked over. She had the dark blue lightweight coat over her arm. The teal silk dress fit just fine, and she looked simply wonderful from that angle. From the back. It had been the thought of Stolen Kisses that broke down his resolve.

CHAPTER TEN

Castle was working. He was out on the street. Studying the sidewalk cracks for a villain's face. Stepping off curbs and looking for clues in gutters. He had just stepped off the curb at Carrall and Hastings when a car horn honked, causing him to lift his eyes out of the gutter and into those of the driver of the bread truck that had almost run him down. The guy's mouth was opened too and he was saying something with emphasis but, because of the glare on the window, Castle couldn't make out what it was. But it probably wasn't "Glad I didn't run you over cause you're such a handsome devil it would be a terrible loss."

He wasn't a handsome devil; hell, folks at the library could tell you that. Castle had no illusions along those lines. Frontenac had the local market on handsome cornered. And he had a good job too. But he was short and unattached. So, then, Castle was not a handsome devil and he lived day to day. What did he have? The only thing he had was Louise Jones. Keep that uppermost in your mind, Castle told himself and his mind replied that it would, and added, You had that post-breakfast drink with Miss Monti so maybe you need a pre-luncheon one, just you and me, over there at the Manhattan Club. And Castle agreed with his mind.

The Manhattan Club didn't advertise. It didn't advertise because it was illegal. The cops knew about it, of course, but as long as the monthly envelope was handed over, the Manhattan Club stayed in business. For nine years it had been handed over. This arrangement only appeared cynical; it was the human reaction to an absurd law. Of course, Castle thought, at least half of all laws are absurd and the rest of them aren't so brilliant either but that's another story. The law that brought the Manhattan Club and others like it into existence maintained that a fellow could vote and pay taxes and go overseas to fight for his country but couldn't go into a public place and have a drink of wine or spirits. A woman could pay taxes and not too long ago she'd been permitted the vote, she could go overseas and put bandages on wounded men but she couldn't get a drink either unless she wanted a glass of fattening beer, and was accompanied by an escort, who was a male person.

You wanted to go to the Manhattan Club what you did was walk along Hastings Street until you saw a big seahorse. It was metal and hanging over the sidewalk at the Only Seafood Restaurant which was the third oldest business in Vancouver, a veritable newcomer really. An entire year younger than Ramona's which came into existence not long after the first suit of clothes emerged from the Seven Little Tailors. Anyway, if you were standing under the seahorse and looked directly over the way, you'd see a green door. You walked across the street, jaywalking like the lawbreaker that you were, opened the door, climbed the stairs to another green door that discreetly announced that The Manhattan Club was on the other side.

Every year somebody put a thick coat of green paint on each of those doors without taking a scraper to the last coat. They weren't careful painters and, consequently, the floors around the doors were splattered with nine years' worth of green droppings. You went there often enough you got familiar with the individual drops. The door knobs were smudged with green paint, green paint had exceeded door jamb boundaries. The stairs were gouged and filthy and they sagged in the middle like twenty-six spavined nags, but only the top two and the bottom two had ever worn any colour, having caught those sloppy drops of green. As for the walls, they were of an indescribable hue built up over the years by smoke and dirt, smudged by padded shoulders and greasy hands, oily heads and dirty minds, and the entire stairway reeked of tawdry hopes, sour breath and busted dreams.

No matter how many times Castle had mounted those shabby stairs, no matter how familiar he'd become with the old timers among the paint drops, it was always a bit of a shock opening the door at the top. Night or day, it was always Two a.m. on the other side of the doors, two in the morning in another land, a land of ebony and smoked mirrors, black leather banquette booths and muted violet light reflected in crystal hanging over the bar like a master had sculpted stalactites in fluted, snifter and goblet shapes.

In case you didn't know where you where, raised letters of burnished aluminum, cut in the steamlined style that Mussolini himself fancied, told you this was the Manhattan Club. And that being the case, it had to be Art Sprague behind the lacquered hardwood counter, familiar part through the middle of his hair. It had to be him because he was wearing a bowtie without looking silly, and though many tried, like the chap at the library, Art was the only grown man Castle had ever seen who could do such a thing. But Art had put on weight. "Art, what'd you know, what'd you say?"

"Sweet Fanny Adams."

"You're certainly looking prosperous."

"I'm looking fat's what you mean. I guess I am prosperous. I own the joint now."

"Good for you."

"Thanks. And because I own the place I can stand you a drink. You're a vodka martini, hold the vermouth."

"That's right. You always had that great memory, Art."

"You been in here enough, for chrissakes."

While Art was making the drink, Castle used the bar phone, called Manny Israel. Manny Israel said, give me half an hour and please come around to the shop.

Castle hung up, thought about Art Sprague's memory. His memory was so good, it had been necessary for him to move to Vancouver. Art grew up on the prairies, playing hockey on frozen ponds and he got pretty good at it. Good enough to play a few games with the Chicago Blackhawks. Parts of a few games anyway. And one of them, in Maple Leaf Gardens, they send him in late in the third period and there's a scrum around the net, Art's off to the side, far side of the goalie, the puck gets away and suddenly it's right in front of his skates, and he has it on his stick and the goalie might have been in Saskatoon, and Art just tips it in. The crowd roars, his teammates clap him on the back. And he never played another game. That was it, 25 years old. Just a little too slow for the NHL. He still heard that crowd. If he'd gone back home, he'd be sitting in the Legion, his mates getting him to recount the story of his goal against the Leafs. They'd be doing it wherever he settled in Canada. Everywhere but Vancouver. Out here, they don't know about hockey, and don't want to know.

Castle and Art met on the Tiny Penny's Wonder Shows. Castle was doing some lip reading for Mr. Extraordinary, the mentalist, and practicing knife throwing with Billy 'The Blade' Powers. Art was a roughie until Mr. Ex discovered his powers of memory and soon had him helping in a bit of business.

"Say, Art. Has the elusive Beanie Brown been in lately? Haven't seen him since I got back."

"He was in yesterday in his corner. Had a couple and got out. Said there was a certain individual he had to avoid."

"Typical."

"Some scotch and water came looking for him but I told the guy Beanie's been a stranger."

"Some thing's never change."

"You're right which reminds me, I could still use a dame like Louise working for me. Like, Louise! There's no dame like Louise."

"Why, Art. I think you've always carried a flame for my girl."

"Well..."

"It's funny to see such a big guy blush."

"Yeah, yeah. Look, she could run the place. No waitressing. I remember the last time you was in we were talking about Louise working in here and, just as I was saying it, old Charlie-boy Shantz made a grope for the waitress's fanny and I realized if it hadda been Louise, she'd of dumped the tray on his head and we'd of been sued. But now..."

"Jesus!"

"What!" Art exclaimed, jerking back his head, surprised by Castle's reaction.

"What you said."

"You don't like the idea?"

"No, about Charlie Boy."

"Oh. Yeah, guy's a slimy party but on account of it's a free country, I got to serve him. He's a boilermaker. Bar whiskey."

"You with your great memory. What do you recall about me and him?"

"I recall, he was with some dames. Manhattans or Whiskey Sours, like that. I think you two had some words or something."

"He still in the same line of work?"

"Private dick, yeah. You too?"

"It's a big field, we're in different parts of it. He was telling me about his part of the field."

"His part of it, the money must be under the rocks. The goniff is always loaded with jack. Works with people overseas. Talks big, Charlie does. And he talks a lot. I shouldn't mention who these overseas people are."

"You don't have to, Art. I know who they are. He told me that afternoon, said I should go in with him."

"That Charlie-boy, he thinks he impresses people with all his big talk, all his aliases. For instance, last week, he says to me, 'Anybody calls for Steve Bildorf, it's for me.'"

"Half the people I know use aliases. And me too. I've aliased myself around the whole goddamned world."

"Yeah, but half the people you know ain't Charlie-boy. You know, I'm just thinking since it is a free country maybe I don't have to serve the guy."

"You served him lately?"

"Two days ago."

"Give me a short beer to chase this."

Art brought the beer, went off to serve a fresh customer who looked like she could have been one of Skinny O'Day's girls fortifying herself for an assignation. She glanced at him automatically. Art said something to her. Castle thought back to that afternoon. Charlie-boy coming from the washroom, zipping up his fly, Castle on the way out of the joint. Charlie boy saying right out what he was doing to make the nut, shipping people back to Germany, important refugees. "They're all kikes anyway," the guy added. Offering Castle a piece of the action. Castle ignoring him, Charlie-boy ranking him as a guy who'd forever be chasing down grifters working the short con.

Castle walking out, hearing behind him, Charlie-boy mutter, 'Screw you, pal. You'll get yours.'

Castle finished the beer, slid off the stool.

"You going so soon?" Art looking over. "You know Janice here?"

"Yeah, and no. Hello Janice. Art, you know where I could find Charlie-boy?"

"He's got an office over there Granville and Robson. It's on same floor as Hurtless Harper. I know this on account of Charlie-boy says he likes to sit in his office listening to the howls and shrieks from Hurtless's office."

"You know where he lives?"

Art shook his head.

"You want to find him," the dame said, "follow the stink."

Manny Israel's store was on Cordova Street, two doors from the corner of Main. He'd given the old place a lick and a polish and that new name. A professional had done the sign that hung over the door and added some touches in gold-paint to the big window, some flourishes and squiggles but mainly a happy couple all dressed up with packages in their arms and smiles on their faces because they'd been to shop at Manny's New Stuff. Castle imagined the happy couple entertaining at their place in south Vancouver. "Wherever did you get that lovely Lazy Susan?" one of the bridge club dames asking. "Why, at this absolutely charming shop in town," the hostess answering. "You really must pay a visit. It's called Manny's New Stuff."

Castle went in. Manny was with a customer. He saw Castle, said, "I'll be with you in a minute, sir."

Manny turned back to the customer, a woman who was interested in a pair of salt and pepper shakers in the form of a Chinese man and a Chinese woman.

Castle looked back at the other couple, the gold-painted man and woman in the window. All at once, he was thinking of Slim Perkins, the bindle stiff who always had paints and brushes in his bindle. Artist paints and brushes. Made a decent living doing scenes on windows, walls and mirrors. Slim could paint anything on anything but barroom mirrors were his speciality. For their mirrors, publicans usually favoured mountain streams with jumping trout, or scantily clad females lounging on divans.

Castle was vaguely aware of the lady asking questions and Manny answering them but most of his mind was in Sedro Wooley in Washington. A saloon down there. One evening there was a big fight in the bar. With flying chairs, tables and bottles. It was a donnybrook worthy of a duster. For once, Castle was not involved. He watched things from the door to the washroom. The barkeep standing behind the bar with his hands up hollering, "No, boys! No! Not my mirror!"

The mirror bore one of Slim's creations. This one combined his two main themes. A guy was fishing at a mountain stream but wasn't catching anything so he was daydreaming. Above his head, between mountain peaks, was a scantily clad woman reclining on a divan.

Manny was still trying to sell the 49-cent salt and pepper shaker set. So Castle thought about how he liked that name Sedro Wooley which wasn't pronounced how you think. Not Sed-ro but See-dro. He liked the name almost as much as he did the one of that place in the Interior, between McBride and Kamloops. Dabney Pridgeon. How'd they get those handles? Maybe Sedro and Dabney were a couple of buddies come across the country together in the Earlies. Castle heard the bell tinkle over the door, and the door close. Sedro Wooley and Dabney Pridgeon. A couple of standup guys.

"What are you thinking about?"

It was Manny talking to him.

"About Dabney Pridgeon, a real skookum fellow."

"I wouldn't know. But I know about the place."

"You do?" Castle surprised, thinking he should know better than to try and put one past Manny.

"My father used to go there with a horse and buggy, making his rounds in the old days. Buying and selling. Twice a year through the Interior."

"He must've had stories. You must have stories."

"I got stories. I also got someone in the back wants to tell you one. I want to help tell to you the same one."

Manny turned the sign from Open to Closed, pulled down the shade and lead Castle to the back of the shop.

On the other side of the door was a room with a refridgerator, cot, hot plate and a table with four chairs, two of them occupied. There was a wheelchair by the back door, a pair of artifical legs lying across the metal chair arms. The legs went the whole route, hips to feet.

Larry Sobell was in one chair, a guy called Danny Klein in the other.

"You all know each other," Manny said.

Castle nodded to Sobell and looked at Danny who took the cigar out of his mouth. "Hello, Gene. A long time. Pardon me if I don't get up."

Klein laughed. A bitter laugh.

"Yeah, Danny. It seems like a long time since the Plains of Tereul but it's only been, what, a year and a half?"

"About. I distinctly remember seeing you there. You coming in to the camp, you and the two Spaniards that were always with you. Two-three days you were there. We said goodbye in the middle of the night. It was early April. The reason I remember it so well, that's a big night for me. I get nostalgic for it. The last night I had my legs. We got blown up just before lunch."

"I heard about it, Danny. You made it though. Unlike Howie Paige."

"Yeah," Klein grimaced. "I made it."

"I'm sorry, Danny."

"Hey, I appreciate you looking sad, Gene. I know you are sad too but don't shed no tears for me. I'm not going to stop fighting. I'll always be fighting, Gene. Fighting the fascists, the Nazis, any other scoundrels and Jew-haters, I can find."

"Which is why we are here," Manny said. "Sit down, Gene. You want a coffee?"

Castle said he did and sat down. Manny brought him a cup and settled himself, looked across the table to Larry Sobell.

"Larry?"

Sobell stopped tracing a circle on the table with one tapered finger. "So, Gene. You were probably puzzled, me walking out on you last week."

"Yeah, Larry. I say the word 'Redman,' you don't even finish your bite of toast, all that strawberry jam on it. Name of a guy you say you don't know causes a reaction like that. Yeah, puzzled is what I was."

"And I told you the truth. I never met the fellow. I did see him once or twice but it was a long time ago and he was, well, how should I put it..."

Sobell looked around the table. Manny finished the sentence for him. "...someone else then."

"Yeah, that's right." Danny Klein interjected. "He was someone else then."

"Okay," Castle said. "You guys all agree Redman was someone else then. Maybe I'm a numbskull but what the hell are you talking about?"

"Of course, of course." Manny nodded his head. "Pardon us."

His skin was sallow. Looks almost like a plucked chicken, Castle told himself. And his hair was sort of copper coloured. It had always been copper-coloured although there used to be a lot more of it. Now you noticed the plucked chicken skin through the copper coloured hair. The rest of him was normal but the hair and the skin made Manny seem like an unusual fellow. Like he was in bad stage makeup.

"He used to be Rosen," Manny continued. "He was born Rosen. Then he became Redman."

"What he means," Klein said. "He stopped being a Jew."

"Something happened," Sobell said. "Made him hate his own people. Maybe he got tired of being called names by the other kids at school. Who knows."

Manny said maybe he knew.

"His mother used to beat him. His father was like a caricature of what the goyishe like to think all of us are like. Hitler needs a picture of a hideous Jew for a poster warning about a diseased race wants to take over the world's finances, he should use a picture of Rosen's father."

"When was it, you saw him?" Castle asked Sobell.

"Fifteen maybe sixteen years ago. In court. One of his times in court. He started out vandalizing synagogues, throwing rocks through the windows of Jewish businesses."

"Then he disappeared," Manny said. "Comes back three-four years later and he's Redman."

"You see him as Redman?"

"No, none of us has seen him as Redman."

Klein shrugged. Castle thinking about Danny's heavy shoulders, big-featured face, coffee cup swallowed up in his hairy hands. Castle almost had the urge to peek under the table to make sure Danny didn't have legs after all.

"Yeah, that's right." Sobell picking up the story. "None of us has seen him but we get reports about him. We have a little group, you see, Gene. Us three, a few others. All Jews, of course. We've been meeting since '35. When Hitler began flexing his muscles, it encouraged anti-Semites all over the world."

"Whatever this guy calls himself, why does he worry you so much. I mean, excuse me, but if he just throws rocks, mails obituaries...."

Sobell held up a tapered finger like he was testing the wind in Manny's back room. "That's not all Redman does. He's graduated."

"See, one of the things we're about," Manny said. "Our little group, we help those people who come our way from Europe. Jews fleeing Germany. Some of these are important people. The Nazis want them back. Redman, Rosen, the way we figure it, he's got to be involved with having them sent back."

"Yeah," Castle grunted. "You know a guy named Shantz? Called Charlie-boy?"

None of them did.

"He's a private operative. That's one of his sidelines. At least, that's what he told me a few years back. Boasted of it, in fact."

"Sounds like a swell fellow," Klein said. "You'll have to fill us in about him."

"Sure," Manny said, "The reason we wanted to talk with you, Gene, we want information on who is actually involved in this trade in human lives and we want to know how it works."

"I find this out, tell you who the bad guy is, the bad guys are, what do you plan to do about it?"

He looked from one to the other.

"You fellows got murder on your mind?"

Manny was looking back at Castle. He seemed ashamed but he didn't turn his head. Larry Sobell studied his hands. Danny Klein's battered face broke into a big grin. "You're in a war, you kill the enemy, it's not murder."

"Forget I asked," Castle said.

"Plains of Teruel wasn't the last time I saw you, Gene."

"No? When was the last time, Danny?"

"Last October, it was. On the Diagonal in Barcelona. When they sent us home. Those of us with the International Brigades. You were with your anarchists."

"That was quite a day, Danny. Dorothy Ibarraruiz."

"I was never no good at pronouncing her name. I just called her what most everybody else called her."

"La Pasionaria."

"'Come back when the olive branch of freedom blooms' ...I can never remember how it goes. Can you, Gene?"

"I forget the words, Danny."

"Sure." Danny Klein poked at his eye with one big finger. Sniffed. Acted as if maybe he was suddenly coming down with a cold. "You think freedom's going to bloom any time soon, Gene?"

"Tell you the truth, Danny. I think it's going to be a long winter."

Danny nodded. Looked at Manny and Larry.

"Please lift me into my chair, fellows. I'm going to strap on my legs and get out of here. Fine bunch of freedom fighters we make. Eh Gene? Two pacifists and half a man."

Just a few hours earlier, Castle's impulse had been to track down Charlie-boy but now he had to reckon with this Rosen-Redman character. Had to consider that him and Charlie-boy might be in competition for a prize called Redl. But, more likely, they were in cahoots. One way of looking at the situation was that he would have to work harder if there were two of them in the game. On the other hand, there being two of them increased his chances of being lead to Redl. Of course, there were now two guys to find before he could find the guy he had to find. And that would make him busier than a one-legged man in an asskicking contest or Jean Harlow in a logging camp on a Saturday night, one.

But that kind of thinking, the thinking about Rosen-Redman and Shantz, was logical only insofar as the premise was sound which was that one of them or both of them had nabbed the guy. And what about the wife? Let's face it, Castle told himself, even though he didn't really want to face it, Frontenac just might be right about her. With looks like that, and talent like that, the world could be at her feet and here she was singing for chump change at a negro afterhours joint in a basement in Vancouver and nursing an invalid husband. Or maybe she was a saint. But saints don't look like that. Oh, yeah, how do you know? St. Francis' Clare was supposed to be a hot number eight hundred years ago. And Mary Magdalene, well, she must have had something to turn the head of the fellow from Galilee. He thought of Galatea Monti out on the town, a five-alarm frail on a boulevard of broken you-know-whats.

Or, maybe she had found true love. Castle had found true love. But what about temptation? Temptation wasn't a sin; it was human, all too human. Even you-know-who had been tempted.

Castle had always liked the way nightspots looked in the afternoon. Somnolent, tired out from the evening before, lazing around until the doors opened and fools rushed in. There were always muted noises coming from the kitchen and a wiry negro man pushing a rag mop, the kind of guy you barely noticed, but you were vaguely aware that somebody was lurking about, poking under the tables with the chairs on top, legs up so it was like a charred forest in the war. Yeah, nightclubs in the afternoon reminded him of that wood near Vimy Ridge, a couple of days later, when the sun was shining and most of the corpses or what remained of corpses had been removed and silly birds were chirping just as if they didn't know what had been going on. Nightclubs in the afternoon with motes of dust in the shafts of window light, a guy at a piano and a dame who made Louise Brooks look like Marie Dressler, standing there singing just for the cook in the back, the guy sweeping up, the owner and the man on the bench, singing in G: "I wandered around, finally found somebody who..."

She hadn't seen him come in, or she acted as if she hadn't, but now she moved her eyes in his direction. "...make me feel blue...."

Then her eyes looked away, stared at the motes of dust and she continued with the song while Castle went on back to the kitchen as if he were a guy on a case who wasn't about to be distracted from his rounds by any trivial foolery or tawdry frivolity.

Raymond Thomas telling him, "Cook's name is Abel Hibbs. At night he's the door man."

Castle remembering how the guy had looked at him curiously. It was a small kitchen with a large wood stove. Two enormous cast iron pots on there. Castle lifted a lid, turned to Raymond, "You on a case, you always got to check the cuisine."

"I understand perfectly."

"Red beans."

"One night it's red beans and rice, next night black beans and rice. Every night we serve it with salad, what you greys call coleslaw. That's his tomorrow night's black beans soaking in those bowls on the table."

There was a screen door that gave on to a small yard.

"He's out there practising," Raymond said.

"Think I'll go out and ask him some questions."

"You won't get any answers."

"He doesn't talk to white folks?"

"That's right. Doesn't talk to coloured folks neither. Funny thing is, I get a peculiar feeling sometimes that maybe he can talk. He just won't. Sometimes I hear him in the kitchen humming when he thinks no one's around. Wonder how long he's been that way."

Castle looked through the screen. The ground was bare around the door, two trash cans to the right side, weeds covering the rest of the lot except for a path between the spruce tree at the left edge of the yard and the spot where Abel Hibbs was standing forty feet away. The yard surrounded by an eight-foot high wooden fence of foot-wide planks nailed vertically to sagging cross pieces. Nailed up a long time ago.

Hibbs took a little step forward with his left foot, his right arm, hand down, easing back no more than a few inches before coming forward. The knife just a silver flash. There was a glimpse of it, maybe, as it left his hand, but you only saw it for certain when it stuck in the tree.

"At least twenty-two years," Castle said. Suddenly hit by a memory.

"What's that?"

"At least twenty-two years since he's spoken."

The man went to the tree, pulled the knife from the trunk. Castle opened the screendoor and stepped out, the man turning around, seeing him, looking questioningly until Castle nodded and then Abel Hibbs' broad face split open in a smile. Castle stepped down into the yard, unbuttoned his suit jacket, put his hands in his pockets and began a little soft shoe routine on the patch of bare earth by the door.

"Pretty nimble," Raymond Thomas said, "for white folks."

Hibbs smiling but watching him critically. Castle danced for at least a minute and when he finished Raymond Thomas applauded. Hibbs nodded but held up one finger like a Churchill cigar, and hit the ground with the heel of his right foot. Paused a couple of seconds and hit the ground again. His gestures telling Castle to strike harder to keep the beat. Then he was showing him, dancing on the path between the weeds. A two hundred and sixty pound man light as a wood sprite. When he was done, Hibbs put one foot in front of the other, bent, spread his arms and offered up a big old darky smile.

"What the hell's going on?" Raymond Thomas wanted to know.

Castle declaiming, "Let's hear it for Ma and Pa and their Plantation Pickaninnies, straight from the fields of old Virginie!"

As Hibbs straightened up, Castle went over and they embraced.

As they separated, Abel held the throwing knife up for Castle to see, raised his eyebrows in a question. Castle lifted his right pant leg, showed the knife. Abel nodded, made short underhand thrusts with his own knife, meaning to say, "I see it's a fighting knife."

He held his thrower out to Castle, pointed to the tree.

Castle took it, held the blade with his thumb laid across the flat, near the tip, first two fingers underneath. He moved his arm back, rotating the knife enough that the edge was down. Just practising taking it back. Raymond saying, "You guys throw the thing underhand? Sharp edge down? That seems all wrong."

Castle threw, snapping his wrist, the blade zooming across the yard, end over end to find a place four feet up the middle of the tree.

They watched the handle quiver in the tree for a moment, then Thomas said, "Now that's right where an average man's stomach would be."

He went for a closer look.

"Blade's half way in. You hardly put any effort into it. Damn, man."

Hibbs patted Castle on the back.

"Just lucky," Castle said. "I haven't thrown in years."

Thomas needed to work to get the knife out.

"I thought it was guns with you," Thomas said. "How long you been acquainted with knives?"

"A little more than twenty-two years." He turned to the big man. "That about right, Abel?"

Hibbs nodded. Thomas said, "Okay, what's the story with you fellows?"

Hibbs smiling, looking at Castle. Go on you tell him.

"Back in '18. We were both with Tiny Penny's Big Dollar Shows. Abel had an act with his family. Minstrel show. Damn good one too."

Abel nodding his head. "They wanted white minstrel shows on the vaudeville circuit, only a couple coloured acts played the big time. The rest had to take whatever bookings they could get, carnivals mostly."

Hibbs put his two big fists together, one atop the other, made what looked like a chopping motion.

Castle nodded, "Abel and his folks, they really were his folks too, used to entertain at ballgames. Negro League games. But, of course, there they dropped the minstrel shtick. We became acquainted in Florida after I got out of the Army, at winter quarters, near Tampa. Tiny Penny took the family on. Abel's, what?—six, seven years younger than me."

Abel held up seven fingers.

Castle nodding, "That would have made him sixteen then. A big kid, but not as big as he is now or I would have recognized him right off the other night. Abel tried to teach me some dance steps, and

I showed him how to throw a knife."

Abel looked at Castle, gently shaking his head. Man, we had some fun and those were sure the days. But then his expression changed. He hit himself on the forehead with the heel of a hand, and he made for the kitchen door. "Look at him," Thomas said, "Dancing up them steps."

They trailed after, finding Abel at his stove, taking the pot of beans off the fire. He went to the icebox, got out a serving plate, ham hocks on it under wax paper. He took two hocks, stared into the cast iron pot until the beans and water stopped bubbling and dropped them in.

"He'll simmer those beans with the ham hocks until midnight," Raymond Thomas said.

Abel smiling. Castle saying, "I got work to do, old friend. You know, I'm looking for the girl's husband, eh?"

Abel nodded, dipped a wooden spoon into the pot.

"You find out anything, you let me know."

Abel nodded again, did a couple of shuffle steps, while he stirred the beans.

Castle and Thomas walked out of there.

"My, my but he's a happy-go-lucky Ethiopian, ain't he, Gene?"

"Sure, Raymond. You stop talking when you're just a kid there has to be a happy reason."

Galatea Monti was sitting on the bench next to the piano player. The man was comping, mumbling something to her and she nodded, watching his hands. Raymond introduced Castle. The piano player's name was Dewey Moore. His nose was smashed flat across his face, big pores in his skin like black holes. He had never done more than say hello, see you later, to Heinrich Redl. As for yesterday, the scientist was there, then he wasn't there. That's all he knew. And that evidently was all he was prepared to say.

Castle left them at the piano, walked around the club. Raymond Thomas came over to him. Castle saying, Nothing personal but his thoughts needed some elbow room. Thomas not annoyed, backing off. The door by the stage was open and Castle went along the hallway to Miss Monti's dressingroom, looked over the contents of the table, looked in the drawers, two on each side, one in the middle. Not touching anything. Surprised there weren't more cosmetics but, then, she didn't need much help. There was the photograph of the husband. The husband in healthier days. Looked like one of those well-off guys who played polo or had flown in the last war, goggles up on his forehead, silk scarf trailing. They had them on both sides. Didn't exactly look like a person Manny Israel said Hitler might put on one of his posters.

He left the dressingroom. No clues in there as far as he could tell.

No clues among the upended chairs or on the dance floor. Nothing more to do here, Castle told himself.

"Miss Monti," he said. "If you're ready now. I need to go to the apartment."

She looked over, said, "Very well."

Not: *Whatever you say, Mr. Castle. I'll do anything I can because you must find my husband—you simply must! I can't live without him! God, this not knowing is killing me!* No, it was merely a subdued: *Very well.*

Castle was watching her pivot on the piano bench when he heard a tapping sound from the kitchen, and looked to see Abel beating his wooden spoon against the doorframe, gesturing with his thumb. Castle walked to the kitchen. Abel glancing over Castle's shoulder, stepping away from the doorway. He extended his left arm, closing the hand, palm up, like he was going to grab a golf club. Then he closed his other fist about a foot above his left one and made a pushing motion in front of his stomach, back and forth, back and forth.

"Push," Castle said.

Abel nodded, pointed to the big room.

"Push. Rag mop?" Castle said. "Guy pushing the rag mop?"

Abel nodded, nodded again more emphatically. Turned his attention to the stove. Castle walked off, bidding Abel a loud good-bye.

"Where's the clean-up man?" Castle asked Thomas, back in the main room.

Raymond looked around, shrugged. "He comes and goes."

"Who is he?"

"Name of Henry Phipps. He's a harmless, quiet kind of man, I can assure you."

"He's quiet anyway. Raymond, I'd like for you to accompany us to Miss Monti's apartment."

"Sure, Gene. Whatever you say."

The apartment was on the third floor. Castle pictured Galatea Monti trudging up those stairs at three in the morning, high heels on the wooden stairs, unlocking the door, the husband in bed calling out, "Is that you, honey?" Of course, calling it in German.

Pictured her in the bedroom that was barely large enough for the double bed and that cheap pine table that held a lamp and her husband's medicines, little bottles of pills, a larger bottle of milky liquid, a glass of water; pictured her taking off her clothes, hanging them up in the closet while Redl watched. Poor guy. The closet was filled mostly with her things; her dresses, her shoes on the floor. Three of his suits hanging there, a couple of shirts. Two pairs of his shoes, size nines. He saw her slipping into bed. Castle wondering whether they had anything at all going on in that regard; thinking probably not, not any more. The actual Galatea Monti standing in back of him, just over the threshold in the livingroom while he dealt with the imaginary one.

When Castle turned, they were facing each other, just a couple of inches apart. She locked those grey eyes on him. He could smell her perfume—like ginger and mint julep—but he couldn't read her expression.

"What was your husband wearing the last time you saw him?"

It was a moment before she answered, thinking about it. "His grey herringbone sports jacket, grey slacks, brown sweater."

Not avoiding his eyes. Backing up when he took a step forward. He looked away from her, scoping the room. Raymond Thomas sitting at the table keeping quiet. What was his role in all this? Castle wondered yet again.

A dresser that was too large to fit in the bedroom was by the door. Two small drawers, two longer ones below. Not much in them. Her underwear that he didn't look at while feeling underneath. His. Towels. A couple of her sweaters in the longer drawers.

Castle stepped to the windows, two of them giving on to Princess Street where a desultory rain had begun to fall. Here it comes, Castle thought. Now things are back to normal.

Redl's armchair there by the window. His pipe rack on the sill, three pipes in their places. Another pipe on its side, bowl resting on a leather tobacco pouch on the sill near a vial of pills. Castle picked up the pipe, fingered it, looked in the bowl, put it back. There were three books stacked by the chair. Castle bent to them. Dioscroides' Herbal, a work on marine neurotoxins, and Notes of a Botanist on the Upper Congo.

Four more books were on the table and, a few inches from the drumming fingers of Raymond Thomas' left hand, a cup that had held tea, which Castle ascertained by taking a sniff, and another cup with a half inch of coffee. "He prefers tea, you're a coffee drinker, eh?" he asked the woman.

"That's right."

Also on the table were two mechanical pencils and a fountain pen with a blue and white marbled finish.

Castle went into the kitchen, opened cabinet doors, looked under the sink, poked around in the trash can.

"Don't you have a radio?"

"No, we have not the money for a radio. We were well off in Germany but our bank accounts were seized. We fled with very little. The money I make is just enough for rent and food and medicine."

Raymond said he wished he could pay her more, and Galatea Monti thanked him.

Castle said he was going to leave now. Miss Monti asked if he had discovered anything about her husband's disappearance, her giving it the faintest hint of irony.

"Indeed, Miss Monti. I've discovered quite a bit."

"What have you discovered?"

Her anxious now.

Castle decided to take a chance, say it in front of them. If they were up to no good, perhaps they might somehow tip their hand. "Well I discovered he was taken from the apartment and not grabbed off the street."

"How do you know that?" Thomas asked.

"All the places on his pipe stand are occuppied and a pipe is resting on his pouch. You told me in my office that there were no ashes in the bowl but if you'd looked closely you would have noticed fresh tobacco in there. Now a fellow smokes a pipe, he doesn't go anywhere without a pipe and his pouch. The way I figure it, somebody came in here, nabbed Dr. Redl and gave the place a thorough going over. They straightened everything up, trying to be real professional, tidied the clothes in the drawers, placed the bowl of the pipe just-so on the pouch.Then they got out of here. It was the work of someone who was a little dumb but not too dumb. He was smart enough to clean up real well, trying to do the job right but dumb enough to leave the pipe and, much worse, the medicine. Miss Monti, the only medicine your husband has, if he has any at all, is whatever's in the pockets of his grey herringbone jacket. He's going to need that medicine real soon."

A strangled cry escaped her lips and, as if she was ashamed of displaying the emotion, Galatea Monti, raised both hands to her face, covered her mouth with her fingers.

"Do you have the prescriptions around the apartment?"

She nodded, hands still to her face.

"How long can he survive without his medicine?"

"Three or four days," she spoke it through her fingers.

"One day's gone. You need to go to a pharmacy, get them filled. Take some pills or liquid out of each bottle, set them back exactly where they were. I'm taking the stuff that's here with me so I'll have it if, when, I find him first."

"First?" that from Raymond.

"Yeah, before somebody comes back here for the pills."

"You think they'd risk that?" Raymond asked.

"They didn't have any trouble the last time. Yeah, they'll risk it. If we're lucky."

"What'd you mean lucky?"

"If they come back it means they want to return him to

Germany alive."

"Then I should stay here with Galatea," Raymond said, "stay here and watch the place while she's at work."

"No, you should go with her to the pharmacy, accompany her to the club. I'll watch the place while she's singing about the skylarks and the moonbeams and the broken hearts, wondering out loud what this thing called love is."

CHAPTER ELEVEN

Castle hit the street and headed west, again fighting the impulse to go after Charlie-boy. He was close to concluding that the wife wasn't a culprit and instinct said Charlie-boy was involved but if he confronted the guy, it would only scare him away. Sure, Charlie-boy had once boasted openly about his lucrative sideline sending "kike scientists" back to Germany but Castle couldn't tell him—Hey, after three years thinking over your offer, I've changed my mind. Sure, I'll be your partner.

Now the way he figured it, Pender Street should have been called Frog Street or Toad Boulevard. That way when you got to Gore Avenue and crossed, it would seem more fitting that the street would turn into a Princess, or vice versa. But, no, it was thrilling old Pender and that was where his building was. He went in, just about five o'clock. Laura ready to go home, looked up.

"Hello, stranger. Where you been?"

"I've been working. Messages?"

"Yeah, you're giving the Bean some competition. Only I'm betting on him when the weekly count is in. Todays results: Beanie Brown 27, Gene Castle 1 plus a postcard from Louise."

"Well are you going to give the postcard to me or just tell me what's on it since you've no doubt read the thing."

She handed him the message slip and the card, "That picture on the card, eh? Grain elevator thrust up out of the waving wheat. What does that make you think of?"

"Hmm, she's getting in tomorrow. But only for three days."

"Yeah, Louise is rushing back, probably got word of the dame with the helmet hairdo."

"Enough about my personal life, Laura. What about yours? The continental dreamboat."

"Talk about thrusting up. Don't hear from him for days and last night the car comes around to my place. No dreamboat in it, just a chaffeur. Guy speaks five words of English. Yes. No. Go see boss. Any self-respecting girl would have told the chaffeur to tell him to get lost."

"But you're not that kind."

"You're right. I get there there's a table set for dinner, linen on it, crystal glasses, candles, swell meal prepared by a servant, lights of the city twinkling, him acting very suave, me thinking—hell, wine and dine me after."

"Always like a girl plays hard to get."

"So we had dinner and then a little this and that and we talked for half an hour, and he sent me home. I probably won't hear from him for another week, or maybe two weeks this time.

"Half an hour pillow talk, eh?"

"Yeah, we're lying there. All these candles on the bedside table. Big ones, little ones. Very romantic. Mostly I tell him about my life. He asks questions. Very curious fellow. He tells me that details, odds and ends, like, can be very valuable. I tell him about my mom and dad, my girl friends. I told him about Beanie Brown, about you. You with your unusual life, the strange people you know and curious clients. That fat man coming to see you the first day. About Beanie Brown ducking and dodging."

"He seem interested in all that?"

"Not very. But not bored either. I'm leaving now. You?

"No, I got some work to do."

"Yeah, what're you working on?"

"Half a bottle of rum and volume fifteen of the encyclopedia."

Nine-thirty at night, Castle's back on the bricks, retracing his route to the dame's apartment. He's wearing his overcoat and fedora. There is a thin and persistent rain and it has turned concrete the colour of a wet rat's fur and made the trolley tracks all shiny. Puddles in gutters reflected prisms of oil and neon like gaudy second-cousins to a rainbow. Bells ringing, sirens screaming, sidewalks crowded. Rain couldn't keep people inside, not here; if it could, Vancouver would be a ghost town for a solid eight months of the year, and a fair part of the others. There was the ringing of trolley bells and the wail of a firetruck's siren several blocks away. Soon came an ambulance's scream, pitched higher than the firetruck's, and after another moment, the still different tone of a police siren. Ah, Castle thought, the city's sweet cacophony, a tenderloin tintinabulation.

A pub door opened and exhaled the smell of stale beer like a drunk's breath. Before the door swung shut, Castle could make out a guy with a chair in his hands, both arms extended over his head and starting to swing down. Half an hour before closing and the boys start to get desperate, thinking of lonely rooms that waited.

Waited unless you knew where the afterhours' joints were so you could delay the inevitable, maybe find something at Annie Tuneheim's brick red booze can to bring home with you or to take you home.

But none of that sort of thing for Castle. He wasn't going to the Porters' Retreat to be all snug and warm, drink in hand watching Galatea Monti as she sang so as to make the gardenia wilt in Billie Holiday's hair. Not for him to oogle as she moved ever so seldomly, making every movement all the more meaningful inside that slinky gown. No, he was going to loiter in the rain oogling her doorway like a callow lovesick youth. Every time a car passed on the wet street it made Castle think of her crossing her legs. But love had no hold on him and he wasn't tangled up in lust. No way. Not him. This was business, Jack. Anyway, unrequited love, as the fellow said, is a pain in the ass. Yeah, that same fellow had added, and it's often a hell of a lot worse if it's requited.

He was on the pavement across the street from her place. He walked to the corner and back, just once, and a cab pulled up, the horn honked. Three minutes later there she was coming out the front door. Raymond Thomas stepped out of the cab, hustled up to her, opened an umbrella, guided her back. Cab pulled away.

Castle walked to the corner again and back, thinking maybe he could change his bearing, his gait, turn his coat and hat inside out so he'd seem to be someone else and nobody'd get wise. Yeah, maybe he'd just discovered the road to riches. Market reversible coats and hats to private operatives.

Castle made six more trips to the corner and back, working on colour combinations. Got to get beyond mundane greys and browns, he told himself. Blue and green might go over well as alternates. You're spying on a house, villian looks out the window, calls to a partner, "There's a guy out there, think he may be watching us."

But by the time the partner gets to the window, the operative has switched to his green colour scheme. Partners says, "He was wearing green?"—"Green? Who the hell'd wear green?"—"Nobody cept the nut outside."—"No, the nut I saw had on a brown ensemble."

Just as Castle was concluding that there might be something to it afterall, add it to Raymond Thomas' line of uniforms for maids and valets, he also concluded his brogans had become wet sponges and his feet were soaked.

Meanwhile, three people had appeared on the other side of the street and none of them so much as glanced at Miss Monti's building. But Castle made the fourth guy as soon as he turned the corner onto Princess. Five-eight maybe, the trench coat loose everywhere except across his stomach. Hands in pockets, brown slouch hat pulled down over his eyes so Castle couldn't make out his face but that wasn't necessary. Only Charlie-boy Shantz had that hunched over crab walk.

The guy didn't even look left, look right, just went directly up the walkway, pulled his right hand out of the trenchcoat pocket and opened the front door with a key. Maybe it was a coincidence. Maybe Charlie-boy Shantz had been given a front door key by some first-floor invalid or a bedridden-occupant on the second, and this noted humanitarian had come around to spoon-feed them chicken soup. Yeah, and maybe all the guys in Pigeon Park have fallen out on account of its Ovaltine they've been drinking from those bottles in paperbags.

Castle kept pacing. The rain had long since conquered his upturned collar and seeped down his back. There wasn't even a tree to huddle under. No trees in this part of town where lived plenty of the fellows whose jobs were cutting down trees. Maybe the men who employed these fellows figured since they spent months at a time in the woods, the last thing they wanted to see when they got home was a goddamn tree. Thus the bosses too were humanitarians. They lived on the west side of town and had all the trees which was only proper since they never went into the woods. They even named their streets after trees: Arbutus, Yew, and the like; there was probably even a Catalpa Street. Very clean and healthy, and their children resembled Hitler Jugen not alley larrikins. On the treeless east side of town the names were harsh and cold. Who could warm up to Jackson or Hamilton?—and even Heatley was chilly. Of course, there was a Princess here but it only ran into Gore.

Charlie-boy Shantz was in there nearly twenty minutes and he came out angry. Castle could tell the guy was out of sorts by the way he scrunched up his shoulders even before the weather had a chance to make him do it. He didn't jam his hands in his pockets either just pumped his arms back and forth as if that would make him go faster. The way he scuttled, bent-legged down the pavement, Castle was put in mind of a portly and sorely vexed Groucho Marx.

Castle kept on his side of the street, half a block behind. Why'd Charlie-boy been inside all that time? If he was holding Heinrich Redl, and had come after the medicine, Charlie-boy could have grabbed it and been gone in thirty seconds. Maybe he was looking for something else. Or maybe the slob had been distracted by Miss Monti's dainty underthings.

Charlie-boy never even looked around. You're a private operative you're supposed to be conscious of a possible tail at all times, a thought that made Castle take a quick look over his shoulder. Nobody there. Charlie-boy didn't even do the store window trick, which is where you pretend to glance at the ties or the caulk boots but actually you're slying reading a whole reflected tableau of the street.

There was East Hastings up ahead. Charlie-boy stepped out into it and a minute later, Castle had reached the curb just as the unmarked pulled up, stopping in the crosswalk, blocking his way. The Scotsman was out the driver's door and around the vehicle before Chief of Detectives Koronicki could get his door open.

"Turn around, put your hands on the roof, lean to it, spread your legs."

That irritating accent.

"But, detective, we just met."

The guy not catching on for a moment and when he did reaching inside his coat, getting his hand on the sap.

Castle muttering, "What the..."

"What was that?"

"I said, 'What the.'"

The guy raised the sap. Not understanding what it meant, he was going to hit it.

"Angus!" Koronicki on the street now. "We'll have none of that."

Castle sighed, took the stance, looked across the roof and saw Charlie-boy disappear. As for the little Scotsman, he didn't waste any time posing as a tough guy, just got right at it. Maybe 'little' wasn't the right word. Frontenac was little. This guy had two inches on Joe, just enough to qualify for the Police Department.

The guy frisked him, rather roughly too, but he wasn't an expert, being too cursory in the ankle area, and missed the blade.

"All right, Gene. I mean, Castle. Turn around." Koronicki talking. "How about telling us what you've been doing the last couple of hours."

"I was on a stakeout and I tailed a guy, and he just now vanished into the decidedly unpoetic mist of Gore Avenue. He's a fireplug of a guy, average height," Castle said. "In other words, taller than Angus here."

The Scotsman closing the distance between them.

"Angus!" Koronicki called again. "Castle, you watch your mouth. And you got to say something to him, call him 'Detective' or call him MacDunnell on account of that's his name."

"I'm hep, Horace. Or, rather, you're Hep Horace."

"Horace?" said MacDunnell.

"Fuck's the matter with you Castle? Every time I roust you, you act the same sort of way. One of these days you're going to step over the line and I'm going to have a partner not as cool-headed as MacDunnell here."

Castle offered MacDunnell a big smile and got a glower in

return.

"You knew a fellow named Larry Sobell?"

Koronicki's question breaking it up.

"Knew?"

"Yeah, knew. He was murdered in a most unpleasant fashion. How'd you know him?"

Castle looked away from Koronicki, his eyes scanning the buildings that looked all sodden under a sky like iron filings, looked over at the Patricia Hotel, remembered before the war, the other one, how he'd gone in there and seen Jelly Roll Morton, the dancers, the tall one who later opened a club in Paris. Called herself Bricktop. They were good days. When he thought about those days, he couldn't remember it ever raining and he didn't have any friends who'd died. He'd been just a kid.

"He was a client," Castle told Koronicki. "Met him an hour or so after I saw you that morning, my first day back on the job. Did some work for him, saw him only two more times. Poor Sobell. We hit if off right away. You know how it is sometimes, Koronicki."

"Yeah, I know how it is."

Castle thinking, We were both counter guys.

"How'd he buy it?"

"The deceased owned a small warehouse over to Clark Drive, little ways north of Venables. Had an office attached to the building, a little shiplap-sided shed with a concrete floor and a corrugated iron roof. Somebody torched the place. Started with the warehouse, fire spread to the office. We discovered Lawrence Morton Sobell bound ankles to shoulders with barbed wire, and fairly well barbecued. Smell wasn't very nice. He was a corpulent fellow and all that fat burned. Yeah, Sobell was still sizzling by the time we arrived."

"Sir, you don't mind me asking," asked MacDunnell, "why are you telling him the details, making it easier for him to devise an alibi?"

Castle answering for him, "Because your boss knows it's not my style, barbecue a friend, or anybody else come to that."

"Don't get too cocky, Gene. We've had a busy night. I'm tired and wet and low on patience. Also there's something I haven't mentioned yet."

"Well I guess you better."

"Thank you. The deceased was a Jewish fellow, eh?"

"Yeah, I know that."

"Had one of them six pointed stars on a chain around his neck."

"Star of David."

"Thank you. The deceased was on his stomach but he'd scratched a couple of words into the blackened surface of the concrete with the Star of David."

"How'd he do that if he was tied ankles to shoulders with barbed wire?"

"Sobell managed to get hold of that there Star of David thing with his teeth. He was very determined to convey a message to us."

"Which was?"

"Which was two words: 'Get Castle.'"

Castle shaking his head. MacDunnell asking him, a bitter sarcastic twist to his lips, "What do you think 'Get Castle' means?"

Castle answering, "Well I'll hazard a wild guess that it means something like 'Get Castle.'"

Koronicki stepped between them, and Castle heard the squishing sound of the Chief Detective's shoes.

"Why was he so anxious for us to get you?"

"What comes to mind, Koronicki—"

With MacDunnell blocked from view, Castle attempted to convey to Koronicki that he wished a word with him privately. The way he conveyed this was to frown, screw up his mouth, and jerk his head to the side, meanwhile saying, "—is that Sobell realized I'd know who..."

Koronicki made his own face, Castle thinking, what a picture: a couple of full grown idiots standing in the rain making faces at each other, and a third stretched on tippy-toes trying to figure out what's going on.

"Hey, flatfoots. Why'ntcha move your Jesus automobile out'n the way so's us law-bidin citizens don't got to walk around it, for chrissakes. Eh?"

This came from a woman whom old age had bent into a lowercase question mark. She had on a rain slicker, fisherman's hat, and the sticks that were her legs rose out of gumboats. Her face looked like mashed potatoes and, as she dispensed more vitriol, Castle noticed dark red lipstick surrounded bits of yellow teeth.

Castle nodded at Koronicki who turned to face the old harridan. "Terribly sorry, madam. MacDunnell, will you please move the car out of the crosswalk?"

The Scotsman, not liking it, did what he was told. The woman continued cursing the police and the modern era as she scurried off down the street.

"Now what the hell is going on, Gene? It better be good. What's this about maybe knowing something."

"Yeah, I know something but I'm not sure what it is. I mean, I think I know something. But I can't prove anything and neither could you."

"Well it stands to reason you go with us, down to Main Street there into my cheery office, and you tell us all you know so we can begin to figure out how to prove something or other."

"I'd rather not."

"You'd rather not, eh? It's not as if I'm inviting you to mount an untested polo pony, Castle."

"Look, Horace. Give me twenty-four hours."

"You know I can't do that."

"Sure you can. Remember what you told me when we were discussing your promotion not to mention your raise in pay? About you owing me?"

Koronicki looked at Castle, no expression. Castle noticed the water rolling around the upturned brim of Koronicki's hat, pictured tiny plastic boats on there. The water spilled over the sides when Koronicki lowered his head and sighed, "Get out of here."

Castle didn't waste any time doing as he was told.

A few seconds later MacDunnell walked up, having had to park around the corner. MacDunnell with dismay staring after Castle, turning to his boss, "What the...?"

"That's what he said as we opened this encounter."

"Huh?"

"You know, 'What the...'"

"I'm afraid I don't understand."

"That's okay, neither do I."

Castle struggled into a telephone booth, water dripping onto the book, found two Redmonds, a Redman and a pair of Rosens. What should he do now? Past midnight and him soaking wet. Go wake the guy? You the fellow that gets a kick out of setting fires, set one today, killed a friend of mine? Guy says, 'Gosh, it wasn't me. Heaven's to betsy."

And how would he know if the fellow was fibbing or on the level? Anyway, every minute that distracted him from the case he had been hired to solve, meant the closer Heinrich Redl was to Germany or to death.

That being the way it was, the only thing left for Castle to do was head for the Rose Hotel, dry off and go to sleep.

The next morning, eight-fifteen in Ramona's, everybody was talking about Joe Frontenac's story on Matty Muldoon, first of a series. Regulars kidding with Matty who was probably blushing but with that lobster-red face who would know? Frontenac there in his rumpled suit accepting kudos and slaps on the back.

Castle slid into his usual booth. Raymond Thomas broke away from his pal Guy Roberts and took a seat across from him. "Somebody got into Galatea's place last night."

"Yeah," Castle said, "Fellow by the name of Charlie-boy Shantz. How do you know?"

"You're not getting suspicious of me are you, Gene?"

"Of course not, Raymond but details are important. Laura, the switchboard jockey, told me her continental boyfriend told her so."

"Galatea phoned me before she went to sleep."

"He boost the medicine?"

"Yeah, but he was after something else as well. The place was what they call ransacked."

"What does she think it is that they were after?"

"She says she doesn't know."

"She 'says'? Am I thinking that means you don't believe her?"

"With her one can never be sure what's going on."

"I may pay her a visit later. When does she wake up?"

"Around eleven."

"Okay."

Thomas nodded, got up and rejoined his partner. Castle wondering how the man knew when the woman wakes up.

Two sips of black coffee later, Frontenac slid into Thomas' place. Large smile on his handsome mug, paper in his hand.

"You read it? My piece about Matty Muldoon?

"Nope."

"Not bad, I do say so myself. I changed some stuff around, polished it since you saw it before."

"Oh, yeah?"

"You want to look at it? Here."

"Maybe later."

"What?"

Castle laughed.

"Ah, you were just taking the mickey out of me, weren't you Gene?"

"Yeah, that's what I'm doing, Joe. I read every word. And a great piece it is as usual. Starting out with the term 'knockabout.' That's pretty smooth, you getting the nautical origin of the term, working it in there, explaining how it meant a rig with no bowsprit before evolving til it was a guy maybe worked on that kind of boat then the word changing to mean a fellow who drifted around working on all sorts of boats. Bringing Matty in but not belabouring the connection. And the details. The bit about the ship's carpenter being impaled not on any old anchor but a grapnel anchor. A good show, Joe. I'd buy you breakfast only I'm flying out the door any second."

"I should buy you breakfast. Afterall, you put me on to the story."

"Yeah, you should but not this morning. Come to think of it, you want to do something for me that might lead to something else to put in the paper you're welcome to. Remember the guy I asked you about, Redman? How about falling by the Byerstock Investments office? He's never there, I hear, but you might smoke the situation over. Then why not take a run out to Fourth Avenue, see a guy called Cyril Fremont hangs out in back of a garage, works for Redman. Go to the sidedoor. That's important. Tell Cyril I sent you, and where can Redman be found. Remind Cyril that I am, and shall remain, the soul of discretion. See if you can dig up anything on any friend of his who might be a pyromaniac. How about it?"

"Gosh, I don't know..."

"What do you mean you don't know?

"Well, um..."

"Well, um? Is that the real Joe 'I Was There' Frontenac whom I hear a-hemming and a-hawing? No, it can't be. Must be his subconscious self. What's his name? Oh, yeah. Timid Tim, pens the Pleasures of Hearth and Home column in The Times. Why the real Joe Frontenac would be up and out of his seat in half a blink of a hophead's eye because he has the gift, the instinct, the nose for news—to say nothing of the contacts—that all the greats have. Take Billy Russell. Yeah, old Billy. He sensed the Light Brigade was going to make that ill-fated charge and it wasn't for him to reason why the hell he should follow them. The boy just did it! And reaped glory. You know who old Billy was, don't you, Joe?"

"Uh huh," Frontenac sighed. "He was the miserable parent of a luckless tribe and I got a feeling you're going to name some of the rest of the Indians."

"Sure I will. Take Richard Harding Davis. Or how about Rory Mason of the Chicago Tribune who grabbed a stagecoach west because he had a hunch that curly blonde-haired idiot George Armstrong Custer was going to roar down on the Little Big Horn. Well, maybe that's not a good example. The point is, Joe..."

"Oh, for Pete's sake, Castle. I'll do it, already. Reluctantly but I'll do it."

"See you around."

CHAPTER TWELVE

Castle had just made the third floor landing at the Trapper's Building, Granville and Robson, when a door burst open at the end of the hall and a guy with a sheet pinned around his neck burst out, clasping the lower part of his face with both hands, and cursing through his fingers. When he moved his hands to tear off the sheet, blood dribbled from between his lips. "You goddamned sadistic son-of-a-bitch!"

A tall, distinguished looking gentleman in a white apron was in the doorway. "Come, come, sir, you exaggerate."

It was Hurtless Harper, seventy years old now, but with a full head of hair though gone white. Castle hadn't seen the guy in twenty-five years, hadn't dared.

"And I should mention," Hurtless mentioned. "That you failed to pay me the two dollars."

"Try and collect it, you sick fiend," blurted the man with the swollen jaw, brushing past Castle and making for the stairs.

Hurtless spied Castle, jutted a manly chin toward the stairway, "Chaps are such babies these days. Whining about insufficient painkiller. My word! When I was starting out, I'd pull incisors from the mouths of bush apes and you'd never hear a peep out of them. Of course, this was before the turn of the century. Real men there were in those days."

"Yeah, and you used a pliers too didn't you, Hurtless?"

The man looked like he should be strolling around Buckingham Palace with the reluctant King in tow, giving him some grandfatherly advice. He reminded Castle of that actor, C. Aubrey Smith.

"I shall ignore the implication sir. You seem familiar though. What was it? Ah, yes. An impacted wisdom tooth, eh? Must have been 1914 or thereabouts."

"That's right, Hurtless and it still gives me pain."

"You're father would have brushed it off though. You're a Castle, yes?"

"Yes."

"Now what were your parents names?"

"Vernon and Irene."

The dentist stared at him for a moment before making a sort of a snuffling sound in his nose.

"Lloyd. That was your father. Always on about the saints. Told me the patron saint of dentists. A woman, I believe. Fine set of teeth your dad had. Never got the chance to look into your mother's mouth, unfortunately."

"Not for her."

"Your father was a polite fellow. Too bad what happened to him. He was in the wrong place..."

"Yeah, I know what happened to him."

"So what's the problem, a nasty toothache son?"

"No, Hurtless. Tell you the truth, I got a feeling I have some nasty business to attend to soon and I'm going to need all the courage I can muster so I wanted to test myself, see if I had the nerve to face you in person. And I'm doing it, see? Now I'm ready for anything."

Hurtless shook his head, rather sadly it seemed.

"I'm sorry, son. But you're not the man your father was."

"You're right about that."

"And what business are you in that is liable to turn nasty?"

"Same business as the fellow that has that office two doors down. Of course, I mean 'same business' in the way I'd describe you as being in the 'same business' as a normal dentist."

"My feelings are hurt, sir. You speak of Charlie-boy Shantz. Hasn't been around for days. I know because I could smell him."

Hurtless smoothed a silver wing of hair above his left ear. His eyes narrowed. The man was gone on a thought. "I'd like to get that creature in my chair."

"I'd like to get into his office."

"I'd wager you wouldn't need a key."

"You'd win."

"Well, cheerio, I have work to do. My attention will be elsewhere, of course. Remember, if your teeth are hurting think of Hurtless."

"Like hell, I will. If my teeth are hurting Hurtless, it's Apollonia of Alexandria I'll think of."

"Childish superstition, my boy."

The dentist went back into his office. Castle took two pieces of wire from his pocket and worked on the locks. It was never as easy as Paul Muni made it look in the moving pictures. But he was inside Charlie-boy's office in two or three minutes.

There was a disagreeable smell to the place, nothing definable and nothing that had to do with musty raincoats or three week old remains of sandwiches. It was the disagreeable odour that put one in mind of unhealthy bodies and bad habits.

Castle started with the file cabinets. It took him ten minutes and he found plenty that was nasty but nothing that was pertinent. In the deep, bottom-right desk drawer were a dozen or so magazines that featured females of all ages and sizes bound by ropes, chains, belts and wire. In some of the pictures men were tied up and women in leather and lingerie were whipping them or relieving themselves on their victims. One magazine was devoted to little girls secured by thin ropes and chains, child-size belts and by thongs.

Castle wondered whether Charlie-boy Shantz spoke German because the text, what little there was in these magazines, was in German. They had been published in Berlin. But maybe Charlie-boy wasn't too interested in the text.

Castle put the magazines on top of the desk and pulled open the middle drawer. All right, that stuff only served to reaffirm Castle's low opinion of Charlie-boy but, like the files in the cabinets, it probably had nothing to do with the current case. Probably, Castle said, because in this business you ruled nothing out completely. Now, you want something has to do with the current case, what you want is right here in this long drawer. An envelope containing three snapshots with a piece of notepaper around them. Three snapshots of

Galatea Monti. She's on the sidewalk in the afternoon out front of the Porters' Retreat. Not in focus, she's starting to walk away. She's talking to Raymond Thomas out front of her house. She's getting into a cab, looking right at Charlie-boy, assuming it's Charlie-boy, who's across the street taking her picture.

The piece of paper had been torn from a lined pad, spiral binder at the top. There was a heading. Under 'Notebooks' were four entries. 'Shine club...The rich Shine...The Girl'— the first three entries followed by an X, and Castle knew they'd been written at the same time because the writing was careful, Charlie-boy sitting at his desk, or sitting somewhere. The fourth was a name, hastily written down, maybe he was walking when he thought of it, reached into his pocket for the notebook, scribbled it: 'Castle.'

What I get for underestimating the guy. I'm watching him, he'd already been watching me. All right, I'm probably more prepared for the creep than Miss Monti is. Time to get out of here.

Castle reached for the magazines to put them back, not watching what he was doing, instead glancing around the office to make sure all was as he'd found it. Most of the magazines made it into the deep drawer but some didn't, hitting the edges, a couple falling onto the floor. Midway through cursing himself for being careless, Castle changed his mind. Complimented himself because the old careless gambit had worked again. There was a passport on the floor. Another one sticking out of a magazine.

The one on the floor belonged to Charles Homer Shantz. Homer? Five foot-eight, 200 lbs., brown hair, brown eyes. Face like some kind of huge experimental turnip. Kind of fitting that he'd be born in Gimli, Manitoba on account of his eyes that could be described as gimlet eyes. Born seven days into 1896. That must have been a bleak day in January. Castle pictured Mrs. Shantz doing the world a favour, taking her newborn out on the frozen lake where the Icelanders were icefishing and dropping him through one of the holes. The icefishers hooking him, throwing Charlie-boy back. —We don't want anything looks like that.

Castle opened the top magazine in the drawer. Taking the passport, he saw that it had been covering the lower portion of a man wearing a mask, ping pong paddle in his hand and about to swing down on a fat girl, no more than fifteen, tied up with ribbons, a few bows on the ribbons, only her ample rear end, where the guy was aiming, unwrapped. Caption over it: Geschenk Gebrutstag! Your birthday present.

The passport designated one Steven Bildorf. The handle was familiar somehow.

Well it behooved Castle to search through the rest of the magazines, which he did, and he found another passport. The name on this was familiar too and, as far as he was concerned, it was worth ten Steven Bildorfs.

All three passports had something significant in common: the photograph of the bearer.

Castle could search for the husband or try and protect the woman. One way of looking at it was that he hadn't been hired to protect the girl but to find the husband; the other way, was that a deranged monster had gotten the husband and now was after the girl. It was Castle's goal to see the happy couple reunited but before they went to their reward.

He hailed a cab at the corner, directed the driver to Princess Street, with a stop at the Standard Building. The cabbie looked in the rearview mirror, glanced over his shoulder, told Castle it sure is a small town. Castle said, Yeah it certainly seems that way sometimes. The cabbie said he remembered taking Castle and some other people to Pier Eleven down the bottom of Shanghai Alley, this would have been a few years ago, rainy day like this.

"Yeah, there was two old people, and a hobo and a good-looking dame. Some other guy was waiting there for you. What happened to all them, eh? See, I sometimes wonder about my fares, their lives, you know what I mean? Maybe I'm too curious. I get it from my Aunt Florence back in Cabbagetown. She'd sit in the window, 'I wonder how old Mrs. McDiarmid got to be so sad,' she'd say. So what happened?"

"Huh? Oh. The old people died, the hobo became a salesman for awhile til he came to his senses, the good-looking dame went to Paris and came back even better looking, and me and the guy that was waiting went to the Spanish Civil War."

"Why is that a fact? Why my Aunt Florence that I just told you about back in Cabbagetown, I remember her writing me the neighbour boy was fighting in Spain. Little Hughie. I used to babysit him when he was a wee lad. You ever run into him, Hughie Garner?"

"Yeah, indeed, I did."

"See what I told you, it's a small world."

Not telling the cabbie about Hughie running away from the Lincolns, deserting under fire. Castle didn't see any shame in that but some might. Physical courage was overrated. The other kind wasn't.

The guy made the turn onto Carrall Street and stopped. Castle telling him to keep it running. He jumped out, traded howdies with Woody, the newsie, dodged traffic and went into the building.

"Hey, Laura. Any messages? I'm in a hurry."

Laura looking up from her board, not smiling.

"The hell happened to your eye?"

"Nothing, Gene. Nothing."

"No? Guess I'm mistaken."

"Yeah."

Laura touched her left cheekbone, gingerly.

"It's that obvious?"

"I'm afraid so. What..."

"Somebody works for the *Times* called a few minutes ago. Says your pal Frontenac needs to talk to you when he's able but he won't be able for a few more hours since he's in St. Paul's because of burns he got over on the West Side."

"Burns?"

"What the fellow said."

Castle turned to go. "Put some ice on that eye."

"Yeah, I will. You going to see that helmet-haired dame?"

"Uh huh. She could be in trouble."

"So could you. Isn't Louise supposed to get in today?"

"Late tonight."

"Think about her."

Joe wasn't going to be chatty for awhile, so it was straight to Princess Street, the cab driver telling him about quitting his job at The Hudson's Bay in Toronto to look for adventure, about finding it, arriving in Vancouver in a boxcar exactly ten years ago, just as the Depression was starting. Unfortunately, Castle had to jump out with the guy trapped in a refridgerator car somewhere west of Weyburn. How'd he get out? Castle found himself wondering as he trotted up to Galatea Monti's front door.

Her third floor windows were closed against the foul weather, everyone's windows were closed against the foul weather, so she wouldn't be able to hear him calling up. In good weather this was the kind of street, if a guy whistled or let out a "Hey, honey, it's me" he was liable to have to duck all the keys being throw out windows by women who weren't fully dressed. There was a flower box on the first floor window ledge, no flowers in it now, just dirt that looked grey, Castle thinking of it as city dirt. He leaned and stretched to reach the box, feeling around for pebbles to toss at her windows, and came up with a key. It opened the front door. Castle asking himself when will people ever learn. Keys in the flower box, keys under the door mat; homeowners leaving a light on, the radio on, when they go to the lake for a couple of days. Thinking thieves are stupid. Castle put the key back in the flowerbox for the next guy wanting to get in.

He knocked on her door and a half a minute later she called "Who is it?" like she'd just woken up.

"Gene Castle."

"What is it?"

What is it? Is she kidding?

"You may remember you hired me to find Heinrich Redl? The name ring any bells? He's the guy who's life is in danger, you're married to him."

She opened the door.

"I was not sure it was you."

It was only noon and she was only wearing what on most other dames would be an ordinary dress but which on her had the effect Dietrich achieved after maybe four hours in makeup and the key light arranged just so.

"It is me. I mean, it is I. Now what you have to do is move out of the doorway so I can come in and look around."

"Pardon me, I am upset."

Castle thinking: How am I supposed to tell?

"Some person broke into the apartment."

Castle looking around, seeing everything as it was.

"Yeah, I know. Raymond told me they ransacked the place. What were they looking for?"

"I have no idea," she said, staring at him with those big grey eyes, said it as if daring him by force of her magnetism to disbelieve her. Then she folded her hands and turned away, took a few steps. Didn't say anything else.

"What was it like when you got back? All topsy-turvy, so to speak."

Castle thinking 'topsy-turvy' might be incongruous given the circumstances and the company but, then again, she probably wouldn't know what he meant. But Galatea Monti surprised him, saying: "Yes."

He began to pace, looked around. Stopped. Aware of her standing close to him. The apartment was not big enough for Castle not to be aware of her standing close to him. Neither was the neighborhood. The city either.

"All the cabinet doors in the kitchen had been opened? The drawers?"

"Yes."

"What about the refridgerator?"

"No. But inside, bottles were on their sides, as if..."

"As if Charlie-boy looked for something in there, got angry when he didn't find it and slammed the door shut."

"Who is this person?"

"The guy who broke in."

"How do you know this?"

"I watched him from outside, then I watched him come out."

"But you didn't call the police?"

"Of course not. The guy broke in here, he knows where your husband is. I wanted to follow him but the police came along and instead of picking up Charlie-boy, stopped me for questioning, thinking I set fire to a friend of mine."

"Fire to a friend?"

"Yeah, a sweet counter guy I did some work for, name of Larry Sobell. But never mind that..."

"I know a man named Larry Sobell."

"What?"

"Yes, a large man. Very nice. The Jewish people here, they helped us with small gift of money when Heinrich and I arrived. They help refugees but must do this very quietly because there are very bad people here who attempt to act like Nazis. Larry Sobell said one very bad man is head of organization."

"This is very interesting, you knowing Larry Sobell. This group, it's like the one you mentioned back in Montreal?"

"Much more evil. They were nasty children calling names, drawing swastikas on walls, breaking windows. These people here, Mr. Sobell and his people tell me, they hunt Jews. My husband, he says, must be very careful."

Castle nodded, taking it in. Went to the bureau that was right outside the bedroom door.

"So these drawers were also opened, right?"

"Yes."

He went into the bedroom. It was his duty. She followed behind him. Stood by the window.

"The mattress was tossed? I mean, out of place, like someone had looked under it."

"Yes."

"How about the closet? Clothes thrown about?"

"No, not much. One of Heinrich's coats was on the floor."

He turned away from the closet. She was fiddling with the blind cord. Opening and closing the blinds. She looked in his eyes.

Castle went into the livingroom.

"You got to tell me what these people want? We don't have much time."

She didn't say anything.

"Notebooks, right?"

Her mouth opened in surprise. Castle thinking it was the first time he'd seen her off-balance. What they called non-plussed only he could never figure out what plussed was. Maybe it was a nautical term.

She took a deep breath, exhaled. Went to sit on the hardback chair by the table that still had Redl's book and pen on it.

"Yes, notebooks."

"Why didn't you tell me? How can I do my job if you're always holding back?"

"Heinrich said I must be careful with the notebooks. They contain all his formulae, the results of his experiments. Do you know what these Nazis want to do with his life work? He made medicine from plants, medicine to help cure sick people. But they want to hurt people with the results of his life work. I don't understand very much but one finds a plant, a little bit of it can cure people of an illness but too much kills them. Yes? Heinich told me they have plans to poison food, water; plans for what he calls warfare with germs."

"Where are they?"

Castle expected the big rigamarole but, no. She came right out with it.

"The black man who never speaks. At the club."

"Abel."

"Yes, he has hidden them. The poor man. But he told me you could be trusted which is why I let you know about the notebooks."

"He told you?"

"Yes, with little pad and pencil he carries in his apron."

"Okay. Now, you ever hear of Charlie-boy Shantz?"

"No one with that name, no."

"Maybe you've seen him. Maybe he's been to the club. Comes up to here on me. Built like a fireplug."

Miss Monti looking perplexed.

"A fireplug. I mean," Castle said, "he's not tall, not short but wide, solid but not fat. He has sort of a sallow squashed face. Kind of like a yellowy turnip. You ever seen pictures of the vegetables they grow up in the Yukon, Alaska? How big they get on account of they get sunshine 21 hours a day in the summer? They don't have many weeks to do it so they rush through their growing, like they're on goofballs. You know goofballs?"

She shook her head, again.

"Well never mind. He's got a turnip face and little eyes. Short fat fingers. Doesn't ring any bells, eh?"

She shook her head.

"Well, let's see, even more distinctive than his face is the way he walks, sort of bent-legged, scuttles along like this."

Castle took a few steps imitating Charlie-boy and when he looked back at Galatea Monti she was smiling. Maybe not smiling the same as regular people do, certainly not beaming like Shirley Temple, but it could qualify as a smile. Non-plussed one minute, faintly smiling the next, really going through a range of emotions. Then getting her face back to normal, saying, "Yes, I have seen that man. He has been to the club."

"What does he do there?"

"The way he looks at me. I feel sick in my stomach."

"I know what you mean. What else does he do?"

"Only twice I have seen him. Both times he speaks to the man who pushes the broom."

Castle nodding. Recalling Abel, making pushing movements with the broom, trying to give him a lead. Castle's nodding was replaced by the shaking of his head, thinking what a careless fool he was.

"All right, I'm going to get out of here, go look for Charlie-boy Shantz, who is looking for me, as well as you. You don't want him to catch you alone so when you leave this place, or return, you have company. Understand?"

"Yes."

"Okay, I'll see you around."

He stood up and started for the door, Galatea Monti following like a polite, if not particularly animated, hostess. She waited until he stopped, Castle about to say—Don't forget now. Don't go out alone.

Then the woman got lively. She walked right into him. Her body suddenly glued to his. All of her body was lively, and it was warm. It appeared Miss Monti wanted to mingle. He saw the muscle in her throat—that fluted throat—move as she swallowed, said, "I cannot stop myself."

Castle, his lips dry, mumbling, "You don't, uh, you don't have to... no inducements are necessary, Miss Monti. I'm going to find your husband."

He was conscious of his breathing. How often do you think of your own breathing?

"You love your husband, don't you?"

"There are different kinds of love."

She gently urged her body against him, face upturned, grey eyes misty. She closed them slowly and he was reminded of her in the bedroom closing the blinds. When she opened them it was like pulling down the covers of her bed.

"I have been fighting this feeling since I first saw you," Galatea Monti said. "But I know I cannot deny this."

Castle thinking, I know what you mean. I know what you mean. But saying, "It's no good, Miss Monti."

"Yes, it will be very good. I can feel that you want me. I can see that you do."

"I'm leaving, going to go find your husband."

He reached behind him for the door knob. Had to look away from her. When he looked back tears were in her eyes.

"Yes," she said quietly. "You are right to leave."

He edged away.

"Just say my name one time before you go. Please."

"Goodbye Miss Monti."

"Not Miss Monti. Say my first name."

"Goodbye...Galatea."

He was aware of saying it hoarsely. For the briefest instant, he could picture his hands reaching for her shoulders and sliding down to her hips.

Castle got out of there. Didn't look back. Down three flights of stairs as if floating in an opium daze. Making the street, not remembering the three flights of stairs. Lifting his face to the drizzle.

Castle put one foot in front of the other. Objects seemed not to be secure, like when they're drilling in the street two blocks away and still your tea cup shimmies. Castle aware of his walking, aware of how he was deliberatly putting one foot in front of the other, like a guy who knows he's had too much to drink but is making an effort to convince himself he's sober as a judge. A judge? Castle trying to think of things to think of, grabbing for images. Him and Albert Batson, Red Batson from Vancouver, surviving that battle in Nicaragua.

Yeah, that's a good one. Getting drunk and carousing in Vista Chica, the Nicaraguan shooting his revolver in the saloon, pointing it at the ceiling in high spirits, and firing. Red instinctively hitting the floor. Everybody laughing then, toasting the two gringo revolutionaries. Bringing them booze. Bringing them women. Well, best not to think about that part. Not now.

Think about Louise. She's coming home tonight. Coming home. The Rose Hotel. What kind of guy was he? He should be able to provide her with a real home, nice place in Marpole, South Vancouver, maybe. Something like that. Hell, she wouldn't stand it for a minute. A home in Marpole? She'd say, What the hell's come over you? You out of your goddamned mind? Hell would I do there? Louise. Galatea Monti. No don't do that, you fool. Opposites, they are. Hell, they probably don't have a thing in common. Thinking about it though, Castle decided, well, they are the same height. Louise a few pounds heavier, telling himself he preferred things that way. Oh, yeah. They both had those great legs, Louise's legs perhaps, well, not bigger, it was more like Galatea Monti's were more slender. Yeah, that's the way to put it. Otherwise, bone structure, maybe a little. High cheekbones but Louise's face a bit broader.

Galatea pressing against him....

"Hey, Gene! What the hell!"

"Huh!"

There was Woody, the humpbacked newsie, at his side. Castle was across the street from his own office. Well fancy that.

"Gene, what are you thinking about? I called you three times."

"Sorry, Woody. Got something on my mind."

"Blonde or redhead?"

"You know me, Woody. I'm a one woman man and she's a brunette. Louise is getting in tonight."

"Good for you. Me, I ain't had anything since the Lindy Hop was in fashion. I used to do my own version. The Lindy Hump."

"You're a funny guy, Woody."

"Yeah, I never miss a trick except that kind."

Castle nodding, "Yeah, what trick of any other kind haven't you missed?"

"The one with the two shines. You know, the two coloureds?"

"How does that one go?"

"Well it sticks in my mind because you don't see many shines around here. I mean, except for Raymond Thomas in the mornings down to Ramona's. So naturally, I'm all eyes. Me being an Indian and all that."

"Reading the landscape like a book."

"Yeah, and with my wise Indian eyes I spy this little coloured guy stop over in front of your building there about an hour ago. And lo and behold, not a minute later a big coloured guy comes up. But he hangs back on the other side of the street, under the *Shanghai Alley* sign. Presses his large dark self against the wall there but he's looking at the little coloured guy. Little coloured guy walks back and forth for ten minutes. Big coloured guy doesn't move. Then the little coloured guy goes a block down Pender, to the west, crosses the street, leans against his own wall, watches your building. Big guy keeping an eye on him. Ten minutes of that, he crosses to the north side of Pender, stays there. Big guy moves down a ways. It's like some kind of chess game on the street."

"So where on the board are they now?"

"Little guy came down Carrall here, other side, turned into the laneway there in back of your building. Big guy came walking right past me down Carrall but on this side. Stopped halfway down the block, stood there looking this way and that for a few minutes then he saw something that got him interested and he dashed across Carrall and up the laneway, and that's the last I seen of him. This would have been five minutes ago, maximum. And that's the crop, Gene. I'd lay money with Beanie Brown their dusky presence is someway involved with you."

"Could be anybody."

"Could be but it ain't."

"See you, Woody."

Castle hadn't planned on returning to the office, hadn't planned anything. If he'd thought about it, he'd have gone to see Manny Israel, maybe, or called the hospital, asked about Frontenac. But since he was outside his building he might as well go in. There was something up in the office he needed. It was in his desk drawer and gunmetal grey in colour.

"You back so soon?"

Laura looked up from her board.

"Yeah. What happened to your eye?"

"We already been through that."

"Oh, sorry. Listen, any Negroes been in here since I left?"

"Any Negroes? What? You been smoking them muggles again? You look kind of funny like you're not all here. Hey, wait, it doesn't have anything to do with the dame, does it? You been to see her?"

"You sure are getting nosey, Miss Easely."

"Gene, listen there's something I want to say to you."

"Uh oh. You've got a serious expression on your face."

"Now, you listen to me, buster. Because I'm not kidding."

"Yes, Laura."

"That helmet-headed bitch is not for you. Louise is your dame. If, for whatever reason, Louise stops being your dame then, well, Gene, it's, then it's you and me, see? Not you and anybody else. Just you and me, Bub. And you know it's true. Don't you, Gene?"

And all of a sudden as he looked at Laura, he realized. Hell, yes. It is true.

"Well?"

"Well, you might have something there, Laura."

"Damn right I do but I won't say another word about it ever, I promise, or until such time as is appropriate."

He nodded and walked to the staircase. That little conversation had snapped him out of it all right. He started singing, skipping up the stairs, "I guess I'm just a lucky-so-and-so."

He reached his floor, and was halfway down the hallway to his office, walking by the janitor's closet, when the door to it flung open, hitting him in the shoulder, making him stagger. The negro man was on him, had both arms around his neck. Castle bent, twisted, trying to throw him off, and the guy came right off the ground. But he had a straight razor in his right hand. Castle seeing it not a foot in front of his face and just to the left. Castle dropped to his knees then and the guy tumbled forward over his head. Hit the floor on his back, simultaneously lashing out with the knife and slashing Castle across the left shoulder.

Castle's reaction was the instinctual one, the wrong one, his hand went to his shoulder, aware of the layers the knife had cut through, aware of his hand sticky with blood, and as he did that, the man, the black man who pushed a broom at the Porters' Retreat, started to get up. He was in front of Castle, on all fours but leaning back, like an animal just before attacking. An animal with a straight razor on the tiled floor under his right hand. Castle was on his side then, scuttling away from the man, who lunged at him, like a wolf would do, pushing off with his hind quarters. Castle rolled. The man missed with the razor, allowing Castle just enough time to rise into a crouch, ready to meet the next lunge. The guy's swing was wide enough that Castle could block it with his left arm, get inside the arc, and land his right fist into the man's stomach. It was a good punch and it would have put down a much bigger man, if the bigger man was softer in the belly. This one only started to go to the floor and he didn't drop his razor. As he buckled forward, the blade caught Castle on the left cheek bone. Castle knew it was just a little nick but it burned and he felt blood seep out. He jumped back, thinking—Enough of this, enough blood. The man was moving side to side in front of him making little feints with the knife. Castle couldn't risk bending to get his blade. He moved in counterpoint to the man, timed his feints, then stepped in, jabbed him in the face, surprising him, upsetting his rhythm, opening him up to a left hook and a straight right that sent the man stumbling backwards, the straight razor flying from his hand. The Negro landed on the seat of his pants and slid ten feet back toward the stairs.

Castle came forward but stopped when he saw the man's hand emerge from his coat holding the automatic. His first thought was of how much noise the thing was going to make when it went off in this narrow hallway. His second thought was of Augie Garmano telling him an important rule of thumb, one the bastard had always lived by, "Run from a knife, attack a gun."

So Castle took a step, thinking: Some attack this is. The guy levelled the automatic, the ten feet became eight, the eight six. Oh, no. Castle thinking, I'm never going to see Louise again.

And the gun went off, louder than Castle had imagined. The noise reverberated inside his head. Something was happening to his head. Stuff was falling on it. And the negro was falling forward, landing flat out, face hitting the tiles. There was a knife handle sticking out of his back. He tried to move, tried to speak. Blood burbled from his mouth and then the son-of-a-bitch closed his eyes and died.

Castle looked down the hallway, holding his hands over his ears, and there was Abel in front of the window that gave onto the fire escape. Abel walking toward him. Castle noting the kitchen apron under his opened raincoat. Abel's big mug split by a big smile. The man looks happy as can be, Castle thought, but not as happy as I am. Thinking about how a man can be happy even though he's got blood practically cascading down his cheek, and he's got to buy a new shirt, suit and overcoat on account of they're soaked with blood from the gash in his shoulder. Not to mention his head ringing. But he was alive and the negro on the floor was not.

Castle started to raise his arms, saying something appropriate like—"Thanks alot"—wanting to clasp his friend, but he grimaced from the pain in his shoulder.

The big man took a handkerchief from his pants pocket, gently touched Castle's cheek wound with it. Castle took it, held it there.

By now, doors had started to open, people peeking out. Castle looked around, "I don't believe it. The elusive Beanie Brown."

The bookie had a round white face, old acne scars and small eyes, one lower than the other. He had always reminded Castle of what little kids came up with when asked to draw the man in the moon.

Beanie Brown nodded to Castle, showing no surprise at all, went and stood over the dead man, seemed to consider the situation for a moment, said, "I'll lay you twelve-to-one, he don't get up."

Within a few seconds, other people had ventured into the hallway, some gasping, others with questions. Castle asked that someone call the cops. Laura came clicking up the stairs looked at the dead man, looked at Castle. "Oh, for Christ's sake, Gene. What the hell have you gotten yourself into now? You're bleeding like a stuck pig."

She looked at Beanie, then at Abel, said, "Get that coat and shirt off him, will you?"

In front of God and everybody else, Laura took off her white blouse and wrapped it around Castle's left shoulder. Then she took Abel's handkerchief and fussed over the cut in Castle's face. Castle careful to avoid looking at Laura's breasts, unlike Beanie Brown who was staring unabashedly with his raisin eyes. But Castle had noticed that they weren't too big—Laura's breasts—weren't small either there in the white bra, lace around the top edge, a few freckles on her chest, thin chain around her neck, crucifix in the valley.

Ten minutes later, Detective MacDunnell came bounding up the stairs, followed eventually by a huffing and puffing Chief of Detectives Koronicki who had stopped on the landing below to call, "What'd we got up there, Angus?"

"I don't know how to describe it exactly, boss."

When Koronicki finished the last part of the climb, he took in the situation, shrugged, "What's hard to describe, Angus? You got one Negro man who is about six and a half feet tall and he's standing up in an apron, another negro man lying on the floor and he is dead, you got Gene Castle here, of course, a situation like this, and you got people who come out of their offices to look including one dame who might have been inside one of the offices taking dictation without her blouse on, and you see all these people moving away from the victim inch by inch on account of the blood that is coming out of him like when you throw a pebble in the water and it makes rings. Only thing unusual I note here is the presence of Beanie Brown who is usually best described as elusive. Beanie Brown who happens to owe me a double sawbuck from the World Series results a month ago, and who I'm going to take in unless he pays me."

"It was self-defense," Castle said.

"You kill him?" Koronicki asked.

Abel thumped his chest with his fist. Koronicki said, "You killed him?"

Abel nodded. Koronicki told him to speak up. Abel just looked at him.

"He doesn't speak," Castle said.

"Yeah, we'll see about that," MacDunnell spat it out. "I'll make the coon talk."

He reached for his sap.

"Don't touch him," Castle said.

The cop turned on him, "Oh, yeah? What're you going to do, tough guy? You don't look so tough right now, as a matter of fact."

"I'm tough enough right now, you little piece of Goerbels gutter trash, that you touch him, I'll rip your arms and legs off, tear your head from your neck and you'll end up as second base down there at Oppenheimer park."

"Yeah, and fuck your...."

"MacDunnell!" Koronicki shouted, "Shut up and get statements, from the witnesses. Better yet, go down to the car and call the morgue. Call the photographer. Get a patrolman down here keep the citizens away. Castle and you, pal, step over here with me. Miss, go somewhere and get some clothes on."

When Koronicki had Castle and Abel to himself, he said, "Gene, what the hell now. I gave you twenty-four hours and you ain't given me anything."

"My time's not up yet, Horace. I mean Detective Koronicki. I still got about five hours."

"Yeah, well, look. What happened here? I mean, I know you got to go to the hospital but still who the hell can tell me anythng?" Koronicki jerked a thumb at Abel, "He can't."

"He can write it out for you on the pad and pencil he has in his apron."

Abel knotted his brows, Castle knowing what Abel was thinking: How you know that?

"But briefly what went on is Abel here, Abel Hibbs, saved my life. The dead man jumped out of the broom closet and onto my back, had a razor in his hand, cut me twice, I knocked him down. He was about to shoot me, got the shot off but not before Abel, who had followed him, threw the knife. I wouldn't be surprised, you try to pull that knife out of him, you'll have a hard time. Judging by the size and look of the handle, I'd say that's a Bowie with an eight inch blade."

He glanced at Abel who nodded. The big man pointed at Castle's shoulder. Castle looked, his hand over the cut, fingers all bloody.

"I think I better get out of here."

"Gene, you see a squad car down there, tell the guy I said to take you to the hospital."

"Thanks. You'll keep old Angus away from my friend here, won't you?"

"Yeah, don't worry. Oh, by the way, we had another torch job today, another body. Had burns but not extensive. What killed him was a couple of slugs from a Luger, a .32. Maybe you knew him? I know you knew his brother what's doing a jolt in Glenora. Eddie Fremont. That's the brother of the dead man who's name is Cyril. And another thing, that reporter friend of yours that's so full of himself. He was there bending over the guy as the guy expired. How come he was there before we were? How come you got something to do with these incidents? Maybe some time you'll be inclined to tell me. Say in exactly five hours."

Castle assumed his best thoroughly perplexed expression and turned away from Koronicki. Abel gave his good shoulder what for him was a gentle squeeze. Castle muttered, "Abel, I got to get hold of what the lady gave you."

The big man looked surprised, bit his lip, finally nodded. He went into the apron, came up with the pad and pencil. His big hand surrounded the paper, the pencil was like a yellow tooth pick. He folded the sheet, stuck it in a pocket of Castle's coat.

Castle nodded, "Thanks for everything."

Abel smiled and waved after him.

There was a squad car just pulling up to the building but the driver, a Constable Riordan, wasn't sure he should take the bleeding man to St. Paul's. Castle finally getting to him, saying, "It'll be on your conscience if I bleed to death staggering down the street."

Then the yoyo tried to show his authority, saying he was going to take Castle to Vancouver General instead of St. Paul's, on account of the Cambie Street Bridge is right over there, you're across that you're almost to the door of the emergency room of Vancouver General. Castle said he had a good friend at St. Paul's and he wanted to see him so they could compare war wounds. Too goddamned bad, said the cop. I got to get back and seal off the scene of the crime. Castle asked him if he played the ponies? Yeah, how did you know? Castle saying, I can tell. Whereas actually he had seen the torn pari mutuel tickets on the floor of the backseat, took a chance they didn't belong to the last criminal who'd gotten a ride. Look, you take me to St. Paul's, I'll give you a sure thing for the fourth race tomorrow. It's a maiden claimer but the horse I'm giving you is a ringer from Cour

D'Alene. Molly Maquires the name. No apostrophe.

"What?" Riordan said.

"Never mind just bet the farm."

"You sure?"

"Sure I'm sure."

"Oh, all right. I'll take you to St. Paul's."

Castle barely got both feet on the ground there on Burrard Street before Riordan took off, anxious to get down his money. Would be a good name for a horse, Castle thought, run her in Pennsylvania. Molly Macquires. He'd known all about the Molly Macquires for a long time. But he'd just rediscovered them in the encyclopedia. It was the entry above the one that really'd gotten Castle's attention: Moloch.

He'd gone up the steps of St. Pauls, there on Burrard Street, like it was the tenth and last round, and he was determined to finish the bout on his feet. He remembered thinking about the final bell ringing as he tumbled onto the stretcher. Remembered thinking I haven't felt this woozy since walking back from Galatea Monti's apartment. And that must have been at least an hour and a half ago.

St. Camillus was there when Castle opened his eyes. He had that big, battered mug, long hair framing it. Camillus was a tough son-of-a-bitch, looked like what he had been: a soldier of fortune. Reminded Castle of Jimmy Christmas whom he'd run into down in Nicaragua. Camillus wanting to cut up jackpots.

"So there I am trying to get over the Alps before the snow starts," Camillus telling him, "and I get bushwhacked, three banditos. I knock the stuffing out of the varmints and I'm back on the path, but all of a sudden another guy jumps out from behind a rock. He's real skookum and almost does me in, never expected him. See I thought there was only the three galoots to deal with. But the lesson, Gene—You don't mind I call you Gene? Good. The lesson, Gene, is there's always some guy behind the scenes calling the shots."

Then Camillus told him about losing all his money gambling, had to get a job as a construction worker. "This was back in '88, you understand. 1588. Yeah, pal," Camillus said, "We both been around, see. We ought to go have a drink, eh?"

Castle said, Sure thing—and the saint went on to tell him how he'd almost bought it on the battlefield and they sent him to a field hospital and he got a load of how bad conditions were. They sewed up his leg and sent him back to battle. One night Jesus Himself was there over the trenches and the breastwork, telling Camillus to stop screwing around. So Camillus became a good guy, hell, a paragon, caring for the sick and wounded, building hospitals. Castle took it all in, said, "Yeah, Camillus, my friend, you're a better man than I'll ever be. Say, who's the dame?"

The dame smiled, her face was framed in white, she wore a black gown. "It is Sister Marie Gorelli, my son. You've been talking in your sleep. It's the medicine."

The focus adjusted and he realized there was a real live nun bending over him but that St. Camillus was just a large oil painting. Castle was on a cot in a hallway at St. Pauls. The sister telling him, "St. Camillus was a wonderful man. We especially revere him around here because he is the patron of nurses and the sick."

"Yeah, him and me are going to have a drink sometime. I need a drink right now, Sister. I don't suppose you'd have a little something stashed around here, would you?"

"Why what a thing to ask a nun," Sister Marie Gorelli said. "You want a little water with that?"

"Back, if you don't mind. I'm dried out. My throat feels like August in Osoyoos."

"Coming up."

Sister Marie Gorelli went away and came back a minute later with a tray and three glasses, two empty, one with water. Took a bottle without a label from somewhere within the folds of her habit and poured a couple of fingers into two of the glasses. Castle drank the water, the whole glass in one gulp, and the nun handed him the whiskey. They touched glasses, her saying, "Down the hatch."

"Thank you very much, Sister."

"One needs a pick-me-up now and again, you know. All the suffering one sees."

"Same in my line of work, Sister. How long have I been out?"

"An hour, hour and a half."

"Oh, Christ! Sorry. Listen, I got to get out of here. I got a friend was burned in a fire. Where would he be?"

"Would he be a good-looking sort of fellow?"

"Yeah, that would be him."

"Third floor. He's loitering about the nurses' station, chatting up the girls."

"Just like Frontenac. Smooth-talking anything female. Never without hope. You'd think he'd give it a rest when he's around ladies of the cloth."

Sister Marie Gorelli, shrugged, "One never knows what might work."

Castle told her she was a real joker, and started getting up. She helped him to his feet and he said goodbye, walked off wearing his fedora and a hospital gown over his slacks.

Sister Marie Gorelli called after him, "There's more where that came from, you ever feel thirsty again."

When Castle reached the third floor, Frontenac was slouched in a wheelchair, gauze wound around his forehead, sleeves rolled up, both forearms bandaged, shirt unbuttoned to his chest, black hair peeking through. There was a nun and two teenaged girls, nurses' helpers, standing about his chair. He looked very Byronic.

"Ah, yes. I carried those two lost little girls halfway across Andalusia," Frontenac said, managing to appear both melancholy and heroic, "before finding a nunnery where I could leave them. Poor innocent lambs, victims of the brutal and tragic war."

"Never heard that one before."

Frontenac looked up, "Gene! What the hell—excuse me ladies—happened to you? You look terrible. I got a lot to tell you."

"How old were those little lambs, Joe? Eighteen, nineteen?"

"This is my cynical, private eye friend," Frontenac said to the women. "We were together in Spain, part of the time anyway."

"I missed the one where you saved those poor lambs, Joe. Like to hear about it though. Maybe you can tell me in the taxi in a few minutes. We have to get out of here. You'll pardon me, ladies, I'm sure, for stealing the dashing reporter. I wonder if you got a shirt, a jacket in the unclaimed items room."

Five minutes later they were getting into a cab to take them to the Rose Hotel. Castle didn't have a shirt on but they had given him a scarf and a sportcoat that was too big for him. His own overcoat was draped over his shoulders. He tried keeping his left eye closed so his vision wasn't distracted by the stitches in his swollen cheek. "So what happened to you?" he asked Frontenac, at the precise moment the reporter said, "What happened to you, Gene?"

"Your turn," Castle said after he finished talking.

"I got to the garage and went around the side like you said. I could see that the door was open about a foot; I couldn't make out anything inside but as I got closer I heard the roar, the sound of the fire. Another few steps and the heat hit me. It was very intense but, Gene, I had a job to do. I'd made you a promise so..."

"Cut the crap, Joe."

"Yeah, so anyway, I kicked the door open and tried to get inside. I could see flames climbing the walls. I have this picture of an electric fan melting. I inched forward, arms protecting my face and the next thing I knew I was flying backwards through the door. The flames must have ignited a can of fuel or something. Anyway it knocked me on my keister. I got these burns but they're not so bad really."

"What about Cyril?"

"How'd you know about him?"

"Koronicki told me."

"Yeah, well, I got to my feet, found a pay phone and called the fire department. Then I went prowling around the outside of the building. Found this guy on the ground in the alley. From the way you'd described him, I figured it was this Cyril character. He was alive but not very, and not for long."

"Did he say anything?"

"Yeah, he did. Said four words. Two of them were your name. He repeated your name. 'Castle,' he muttered it. 'Castle.' Like he was strangling."

"Poor guy. He was burned, eh?"

"Maybe a little."

"What'd you mean a little? He's dying there in the alley."

"Yeah, from gun shot wounds."

"What were the other two words?"

"It doesn't make sense what he said."

"Well, what the hell, Joe. Maybe they'll make sense to me. Tell me for chrissakes."

"He says, 'Castle, Castle. Mister Death.'"

"'Castle, Castle. Mister Death.'?"

"Yeah, it make sense to you?"

"No."

"Mister Death." Frontenac repeated it. "What the hell did he mean?"

"Did you tell that to Koronicki?"

"No way."

"Good. First we have Larry Sobell scratching out 'Get Castle.' Now this, 'Castle, Castle. Mister Death.' He'll think I'm Mister Death."

"Maybe that's the message. Person gets involved with Castle, he, or she, winds up dead."

"You're still alive, aren't you, Joe?"

"Yeah, but it's only 8:30."

They continued the conversation in the room at the Rose Hotel. Castle in singlet and shorts, the sportcoat around his shoulders, in bed, leaning against the headboard. Frontenac in the straight-back chair, down near the end of the bed, feet on the mattress.

Frontenac was saying, "So if you're not Mister Death, who the hell is? The most obvious suspect is Redmond, who used to be Rosen, right?"

"If it's Redman-Rosen, also known by three or four other names, why didn't Cyril just say it? He wanted me to know, you'd think he'd have just said 'Redman'."

"Except who know's what it's like to be dying in an alley? What a person's thinking about. The mind's playing tricks on you, your subconscious kicking in there. Like with Durutti, eh? Famous anarchist fighter, bank robber, assasin. Last words, remember?: 'Elegant damsels in Hispana-Souzas get Leandro.' The hell kind of thing for an all-around, tough son-of-a-bitch like that to say? Say, maybe it's the elegant damsel in this case."

"I thought of that before. Only I was with her at the time."

"You were? You son-of-a-gun."

"Nothing like that, Joe."

"Yeah, yeah. How about your pal, Raymond Thomas?"

"I thought about him too."

"Cyril know him? Know of him?"

Castle shook his head.

"Okay, that's one thing. Then you consider he's around the dame all the time. Maybe he wants her all to himself. Sure she's white and he ain't, and they're not going to go live happily-ever-after in Marpole or any place like that but down here in the tenderloin, nobody'd much care. Somebody finds the husband dead, they don't find the killer. So? Too much killing going on in town anyway. Not enough time to investigate every case with proper dilligence. Things blow over, Galatea and Raymond cease their ducking and dodging. How does it listen, Gene?"

"It listens good, Joe. Maybe too good. But why would he have to kill Larry Sobell and Cyril Fremont?"

"Well you said the dame told you Sobell was part of a group that helped them out upon their arrival in town. Maybe there's a connection somewhere with Redman. He's a jew pretending not to be. Hates what he really is. And as for Raymond Thomas. What do you really know about him? I mean except for his connection to Guy Rogers? And that's more than passing strange when you think about it, eh?"

They both heard the doorknob being turned.

Castle reached behind him to get his revolver from under the pillow, bringing it out and pointing it at the door. Frontenac jerked backward and the chair fell over. He was flat on his back when the door opened.

Louise Jones was standing there, suitcase in one hand, key in the other. The gun pointed at her.

"Jesus, honey. Don't shoot me. I'm only three hours late."

Castle sighed and let the gun down onto his lap.

She looked at where he'd put it, mumbled, "One thing pointing at me's enough. I don't need two. Or three," she added, glancing at Frontenac on the floor, one foot up on the overturned chair, and back at Castle. "Dont bother to get up, Gene."

"Christ, am I glad to see you, Louise."

"Yeah, I can see all hell breaks loose, I'm gone for a week. Seriously though, you guys, I mean is this a room in the Rose or goddamned St. Paul's?"

"We exchanged one for the other today," Frontenac told her, getting up from the floor, upending the chair, offering it to her.

"Thanks but I think the bed is what I want. For more reasons than one. I need a rest from them boards."

Louise sat at the foot of the bed. "But before Joe skedaddles, I suppose you gents ought to tell me what's been going on. I guess it's been pretty dull without me."

"Sure has, honey. But I should let you know right away, you got one more turn to do before you have your rest."

"Oh, yeah?" she said.

"Oh, yeah? said Frontenac.

Castle nodded.

"And when do I take the stage?"

"Tonight. Or, rather, this morning, about three."

"That's the time for romance and regrets," Louise mused.

"Yeah, and danger too," Castle said.

"A beautiful dame's involved," Frontenac interjected. "And that's an understatement."

Louise crooked an eyebrow at Castle, "A beautiful dame, eh? Is that so, Gene?"

"Well, Louise. You'll see for yourself in a short time."

"Now, Gene. That's not good enough."

"If I were to be perfectly honest, Louise..."

"Aren't you always?"

"I'd have to admit that the woman in question, well, let me just say, we're not talking about Margaret Dumont here."

Half an hour later when they were done telling the tale, Frontenac got up from his chair and got out of there. Louise, lying across the bed, waited to hear the door close, made sure it wasn't going to open again on account of Joe Frontenac forgetting his hat, said, "You don't look like you're capable of the usual acrobatics, Gene. So you just lie right there where you are."

She closed the space between them on her hands and knees. Got one knee on either side of him. "A beautiful woman, eh? Well," she lowered herself onto Castle's lap. "I'm going to show you all you need to know about women, buster."

CHAPTER THIRTEEN

Castle groaned, knowing with a part of his mind that there was a door and someone was knocking on it. But it felt quite good where he was, delicious, in fact. His body and the mattress, they were in perfect harmony. Louise was at his side asleep, so it was three-part harmony. The knocking continued. The beat took a form. Rap rap. Rap rap. Quiet yet firm and insistent. Castle reached under the pillow but the gun wasn't there. He groped for it. Thought of calling out, "Just a minute while I find my revolver."

Louise was lying with her back back to him, knees bent and the gun was on the mattress in the crook between her rear end and the back of her calves.

She woke as he reached for the gun, muttered, "Huh?"

"Yeah?" Castle called, "Who is it?"

Castle's mouth felt like it was full of oats that might have been shot from guns but hadn't been cooked yet.

"Yass, boss. I got heah a message for ya."

"Where you from? A minstrel show?"

"No suh, no suh."

"Why don't you slide it under the door?"

"No suh, caint do that. Cause it ain't written down, cause I'se posed to delivers it personally."

Castle looked to Louise, nodded at the door. She knew what to do. They'd been through this sort of thing before.

Louise grabbed her coat from the floor, put it over her shoulders and went to the side of the door. She reached across, grabbed the knob, turned it and pulled the door to her, and the man standing in the hallway was looking at the barrel of Castle's revolver.

"Damn, man," said Sam Case, railroad porter and trumpet player. "Please put that thing down, man."

For the second time in an hour and a half, Castle dropped the gun in his lap and sighed.

"What's with the Uncle Remus routine, Sam?"

"I figured if I sounded humble you'd be sure to open the door. Ma'am," he said, nodding at Louise. "I mean, you might of been suspicious being as how you already had one dusky brother who wasn't so humble try to kill you today, what I heard."

"Yeah, and another of your persuasion saved my life."

"And he's why I come to see you, Gene."

Castle told Sam to come in and have a seat. Sam sat on the hardback chair.

"Something's happened to Abel?"

"I'm afraid so."

"Something bad?"

"As bad as it gets."

"I got to get over there."

"No, Gene. You got to stay here cause the cops are there. Raymond says you wouldn't want them to see you. I come to tell you and to keep you away."

"Raymond's right. What happened?"

"None of us heard a thing. It was me went back to the kitchen for some beans and rice. I always like to have my dinner bout two hours before playing but Abel don't like none of us serving ourselves from his pans. He wasn't in the kitchen so I knew he had to be in the yard. I called out to him, 'Abel!' I said, 'You stop messin with them knives now, Hibbs. Come in here and give me some food, man.' Oh, Lord have mercy."

Sam slumped forward in the chair, elbows on his knees, clasped his head between his hands. After a moment, he looked up.

"You know that tree he was always throwing knives against?"

"Yeah."

"Uh huh. Abel was tied to it with barbed wire. Bleeding from dozens of places where the wire cut into him. Not only that.

Somebody cut off his hands."

"Oh, Jesus, God!" Louise exclaimed.

"Yeah, both hands."

Castle swallowed hard and blinked his eyes as if he was both fighting back tears and trying to erase the image that Sam proceeded to paint more clearly.

"Blood was just dripping from where his hands used to be. One hand on the ground there at Abel's feet. Didn't see the other hand anywhere. Gene, I know you're supposed to find the scientist but what about the man who done this?"

"I'm going to find him too. You bet I will."

"Yeah, man but there's something you got to consider."

"What is that, Sam?"

"I thought about it when I rushed out there to Abel. What I thought about was the man who done this. Abel, he was a big man and he was tough. More than tough. And he had that way with the knives."

"What are you getting at, Sam?"

"The man who done this, he was able to take those knives away from Abel, tie the big man up, cut off his hands. That must be some kind of man. I wouldn't want anything to do with no man like that. Would want to see what he looked like though. You have any idea who it could be?"

"Yeah," said Castle. "I never seen him but I know who did it. Know what he's called."

"What's that?"

"He's Mr. Death."

"I never met this Abel Hibbs," Louise said. "But I can't help thinking of the poor man out there suffering like that, never saying a word. You said he didn't speak, eh Gene?"

"Yes."

"That there's what's really strange," Sam Case said. "I never heard Abel say a word. Nobody I know ever heard him say a single damned thing. Well when I got out there to the tree, his head was hanging down. I thought he was dead, you know but in case he wasn't I needed to see if there was anything I could do. I lifted Abel's head. He looked at me, man. I ain't never going to forget the way he looked at me, his eyes bulging, his tongue sticking out. And if I wasn't scared enough already, he spoke."

"Abel spoke?"

"Yeah, Gene. He looked right at me and what he said, it don't make sense."

"Well what the hell did he say, Sam?"

"He said, 'Princess and Gore.'"

CHAPTER FOURTEEN

The guy had done the intro, the lights were dimmed, the quintet vamped the tune, Sam Case trading riffs with the beanpole sax player and, after sixteen bars, the spot hit the mike at the center of the stage, and from the right, Galatea Monti in a shimmering indigo gown cut on the bias, came gliding toward it. She stood stock still, arms straight down, palms flat against her thighs, and sang: "It had to be you..."

Frontenac saying, "I felt that all the way down to my toes. Oh, Lord God why didn't you make me six feet tall?"

Raymond Thomas turned toward Frontenac, giving him the Keep-it-down look.

Castle thinking about how many times he'd heard the song, and everyone sang the phrase without a break, everyone singing it straight and straight through. Only Billie Holiday putting that twist on 'you,' the way she'd done on some record with Teddy Wilson back in '36. And after that you heard all these other singers getting cute with the 'you.' Even guy singers. But Galatea Monti went her one better, singing the first two words straight out then pausing for a full beat, the "to be you," coming out like an exhalation, a bittersweet murmur of resignation.

Castle thinking all this, then looking up, seeing Louise watching the woman closely, studying her. Louise biting her lower lip.

Galatea Monti singing about wandering around, finally finding someome who could make her feel blue, but that same fellow could also give her a thrill. The woman never moved, just stood there in front of the microphone and stared above the heads of the crowd in the Porters' Retreat, at some spot on the far wall. Not a vacant seat in the joint this night. Only some of the audience aware they were eating Abel's last meal.

When Galatea Monti finished the number, the last phrase being the same as the first, she never moved her body, hardly moved her head, but those big grey eyes turned from whatever had held her attention on the back wall, and flicked over to the table where Castle sat with Louise, Frontenac and Raymond Thomas. This in the instant before the applause broke out. With her there was always a moment before they started clapping. And then her eyes were on the crowd, acknowledging the applause.

Louise had glanced at Castle when the woman looked over. Gene catching it in his peripheral vision. But, simultaneously, Raymond Thomas had broken out in a smile, nodding at the stage. Louise seeing this too, looking from Raymond to the woman.

"You're right," Louise said to Castle. "She doesn't resemble Margaret Dumont."

The next tune was "When Lights Are Low" and she kept on straight through a string of six more songs, no recognition of the audience except for the almost cursory nods and half smiles in between numbers. No more than that when they gave her a standing ovation on "If I Could Be With You One Hour Tonight." Or again after the last number, what Castle figured was her signature piece:

I'm a girl who likes to mingle
Soft lights and scintillating
Conversation that's what I like
Especially late at night
Ooh, it gives me such a tingle
All over...

They exclaimed out loud after the *mingle* and the same after the *tingle* and they went wild after the *all over*. But she glided off just as cool as can be. As if she hadn't just set certain imaginations aflame and stirred up envy in many a heart. No, it was as if the woman hadn't a care in the world. In fact, she'd have been sure to win a vote for the woman in the joint least likely to have a kidnapped husband being held captive by at least one homicidial maniac.

Raymond got up to see she wasn't bothered. His sister's kid, Renny Weeks was stationed outside her dressingroom door. Renny had wanted to be a football player until Joe Louis won the title. Now he wanted to be Joe Louis. So far he was 6 and 0.

"What do you think?" Castle said after she'd left the stage.

"About her?"

"You know what I mean."

"I have, of course, done all types."

"You certainly have, Louise."

"Yeah, but all those women, Hedda Gabler, Stella Dallas, etc. They were all real woman."

"What'd you mean?"

"I mean that bitch that was up there, she ain't normal."

"I don't understand you, Louise."

"The hell you don't, Gene."

"You going to do it?"

"Damned right I am. I'm staying right here, watching every set. Not taking my eye off that damned Cleopatra."

"Good. I'm going to leave and round up what I need for my part. Go over to the Manhattan and get Art. He'll do anything for you, Louise. Put Frank in place, give him his piece."

"Frank Evans?" Frontenac said. "I thought he was on the wagon and selling vacuum cleaners."

"You can't keep an old Wobbly on the wagon. You should know that. I ran into him working with a pick and shovel and a hangover on the new viaduct project. 'What happened?' says I. 'Well, I dreamed I saw Joe Hill last night,' says he. 'What did Joe want?' says I. 'Joe wanted to know what the hell I thought I was up to.'"

"I'll have to interview him later. If there is a later. You think he'll be sober tonight?"

"He better be. Now you two got it straight, eh? When the last set's done, Joe you get the notebooks, come back to the table, then you and Louise go to her dressingroom. Until then and under no circumstances are you to tell anybody where the notebooks are."

"How can I? You haven't even told me yet."

From the inside jacket pocket of his suit, Castle brought the note Abel had written for him, unfolded it, laid it on the table.

"At the bottom of the woodbox?" Frontenac exclaimed.

"Keep it down for Chrissakes," Louise hissed.

"I been back there and checked." Castle whispered, "You're looking at the stove, the box is on the right hand side. The two notebooks are on the bottom at the back. Any questions?"

"What about the dame?" Louise asked. "She know what she's supposed to do."

"She knows what she's supposed to do. Let's just hope she does it. Raymond supposedly gave his nephew, that Renny Weeks kid, his instructions."

"But" Frontenac interjected, "We're not sure about Raymond."

"We'll be sure about him soon enough, one way or the other."

An hour later, Castle was sitting on a chair looking out a window through beaded curtains and Lily Dunleavy was adding a tot to his half cup of tea.

"That's it for me, Lily. Got work to do."

She set the rum bottle on the fake oriental rug that covered the table with the crystal ball on it, and pulled up a chair. Looked where Castle was looking, not knowing what he was looking at, her bracelets and earrings jingling.

"You always were getting yourself into crazy situations, Gene."

"Me?" he said with mock dismay. "You should talk. I used to know a nice Irish girl from the Point in Montreal. Sure she ran away from home and joined the carnival but she usually managed to go to mass on still dates."

"Not often. Most of those towns were run by Orangemen."

"Then I turn my back and Lily's gone. Madame Hanska in her place."

"Turned your back for eighteen-nineteen years."

"You're still a looker, Lily."

"Yeah, for a middle-aged broad."

"For any kind of broad."

"Had to dye the hair black. You pretend to be a gypsy who got to have black hair. Otherwise, it's all the legitimate me. Whatever that's worth. I heard you got hitched."

"No such thing. Got me a steady date though. Louise Jones, remember? Was a kooch girl with Tiny Penney?"

"Oh, yeah. I spent part of a season with Tiny. Louise was, uh, shall I say, curvaceous? Yeah, when she walked across the lot the only thing missing was the guy on the drums, bump bump do bump."

"That's her. And how about that long time beau of yours, the grifter's grifter, Terry Sparks?"

"Long time since I seen him. Long time since anybody's seen him unless its the devil or the worms."

"Sorry. How'd he buy it?"

"Took three slugs in Queens Park, Toronto."

"Come on, Lily. I got to pull teeth here?"

"Pigeon drop went awry. The mark's old man did it, and I mean 'old' man. She being a seventy year old broad herself. The meet after the set up happens. She brings Father Time, he looked like, with her. And he plugs Terry. Expired right there under the statue they got there of somebody or other. I beat it before the flatfoots caught the squeal."

"Well that's too bad, Lily."

"It was long overdue but at least it was a fitting end for a guy worked the short con all his life."

"Thing I remember most about Terry, he was a silver-tongued devil."

"Yeah, you might find this hard to believe but I was there in Saskatoon, this would of been in '24, he worked the Romanian box trick on a feed salesman from Manyberries."

"Jeez, I thought the last time anybody put that over. Jem Mace was the champion."

"He was my man, Terry."

"And my man across the street, he just tipped me the wink. So I'm going to get out of here in about ten seconds."

"Come back anytime."

"Sure, Lily. Say, you ever laid eyes on the girl sings at the club over there?"

"Sure, I finally seen her the other day. I'm always looking out the window watching everybody come by my joint without so much as a glance and turning in to hear her. I seen her in the afternoon when she's over there for rehearsals."

"You ever see her up close?"

"Not too close on account of I'm supposed to be a gypsy and so is she and if she is a real one and I meet her she might blow my gaff."

"I'm hep. Is that her coming out now with the Negro guy?"

"Separate those beads a little more."

"There. She's stepping into the light now from the street lamp. Take a close look, Lil. I need to be sure."

"Oh, yeah. The cape is new but who the hell else has a hair-do like that? The frail's got good gams on her, I'll say that."

Castle finished his toddy and stood to go. Lily took his cup, looked into it.

"You going to read the leaves, Lily?"

"I already read them, Gene."

"You going to tell me the future?"

Lily didn't answer.

Castle knew what that meant. Knew the code. You were in the know and you saw a comrade's future, especially something bad, you lied your head off.

"Come on, Lily."

"You're going to make a million, marry the girl of your dreams, and have a daughter who grows up to be Prime Minister."

"I always figured things would turn out like that. See you around."

"Sure, Gene. See you around."

After he'd gone out the door, Lily adding, "I hope."

The rain had stopped. It was misty. A bit of fog. Raymond Thomas and Frontenac walking with the woman between the buildings, then flanking her on the sidewalk. Castle hanging back on the other side of the street. When they'd gotten to the pavement outside the club on Homer Street, there were guys waiting for a close up look at her. A couple of them actually extended autograph books, and she'd signed them.

He studied her deceptive walk, how slow it looked but wasn't slow at all. Like she was gliding in three-quarter time but still somehow staying right with the men. Right in step with Raymond anyway, only Frontenac seemed to be hurrying. Whenever they were near a street lamp, the backs of her legs were like flashes of mercury.

Castle's eyes would dart away to scan the street. He looked in every doorway, at every parked car.

When they'd gone a block and a half north, Frontenac turned east on Robson Street, waved good night. Castle could hear him calling, "Don't let those notebooks out of your sight."

The reporter strolled away like a guy without a care in the world, hands in pockets singing in a loud monotone about a girl who likes to mingle.

The Bay occupied an entire block, and the back of it ran along the east side of Homer. There were dozens of painted-over windows, a couple of sealed doorways and a dreary shoppers' entrance that might have been designed to make you feel like you weren't good enough to go in the front way. There was also a cobbled driveway for trucks that lead back to loading ramps. Earlier, going over the route, this is what had worried Castle the most.

Now, he was watching the driveway, watching closely. They passed one of the boarded-up doors and stepped out into the driveway. Castle had his hand at the back of his waistband, gripping the gun. But nothing happened. The two of them made the curb.

Castle had just taken his hand away from his piece, when he noticed a shadow behind them and saw the shadow turn into a man, a big man who stepped onto the pavement from the sealed up entrance they had just passed.

"Hey, Miss Monti!" he called. "I seen your show twice this week already. You're swell Miss Monti."

They stopped and looked back.

Castle thinking, if he were a bad guy, he would have made his move when they walked by him at the entrance.

"Thank you so much," she called. Castle picking up on the accent in the still street.

"Hey, Miss Monti?"

Castle stood at the side of a '37 Chrysler, the roof hiding everything but his face, forehead and fedora. The guy's voice sounded young and somehow sounded familiar.

"Yes, what is it?" she said.

Castle watched the guy take hold of his crotch, "How about you lose the nigger, come get some of this?"

Raymond Thomas took a step toward the guy, another step. Castle whispering, saying: No, don't do it. Don't do it.

"Yeah, bitch," the guy calling. "You like going down on that boot?"

One more step and Raymond was in the driveway. Castle heard the motor rev, just as the guy was saying, "Come on, coon. You want to try me?"

Raymond was in the middle of the cobbled driveway when the big sedan leapt forward and hit him, knocked him twenty feet out into Homer Street.

Castle came running from half a block away. The passenger door opened, Castle recognizing the man who got out and shouted to the one on the pavement. "Grab the broad for chrissakes."

She wasn't going very fast. The tight dress and heels.

Castle taking his eyes from her to see Raymond Thomas trying to get to his feet. Raymond on his knees. He was lifting his hands like he was going to pray when the sedan slammed into him again and kept going, the front wheels rolling over his legs. The driver backed then, backed over him and his scream was smothered by the fog.

The next noise was the guy he recognized, shouting, "Bring her the fuck back here."

Then a shot rang out, breaking a painted-over store window, ten feet from the head of the fireplug of a man who'd gotten out of the car.

Frontenac was at the corner where he was supposed to be, arms across the hood of a car, getting off another shot now. Good old Joe, surprising him. The taller man let go of his quarry, started for Frontenac. He managed a couple of strides before the reporter shot him in the leg. The other guy grabbed the woman. One arm around her neck, the other with a rod. He let off a shot but Frontenac was hunkered down not giving him anything.

The car rolled up between the two shooters. It was pointed north, ready to go. Castle kept coming forward, staying behind cars on the other side of the street, same side as Frontenac, dashing across open spaces in a crouch. Two of them now moving in a crouch.

He stopped when he was adjacent to the car in the street, adjacent to the passenger side. The barrel-shaped man was dragging her toward the car, shielding himself with her. His partner was rolling around on the pavement, holding his knee, whimpering and cursing like a mean baby. Raymond Thomas was still on his stomach.

Castle stared down the pavement at Frontenac, each of them behind a car, willing him to look over. He didn't do it. Castle made a dash for the sedan. A Packard with a dented rear fender, recognizing it from the garage. Realizing who the tall guy was who'd stepped out of the entrance, started this rolling. Bob was his name. Maybe reluctant Bart was behind the steering wheel. Well, I'm going to find out.

Castle heard his own shoes on the wet asphalt but no one else did. Certainly not the driver. It was Bart, all right. Castle kneeling down there by the running board, peeking in. Bart with his piece against the steering wheel. Castle took a deep breath. Clubbed the window with the butt of his gun. Bart jerked his head around, them locking eyes for an instant. A flash of a second that would be suspended in memory ever after. Bart's face in a million pieces through broken glass. Castle lowering his head before they both fired. Castle shooting into the car, not looking, their shots mingling, and then Castle aware he was the only one firing. Time to raise your head, he told himself, and pulled the trigger one more time. Hearing nothing but the click.

He took the knife from its ankle sheath, peered in through the smoke. He could make out Bart's wiry brushed-back hair, the tip of his nose, maybe a bit of chin, the rest of him was a mass of blood and pulp. Blood already soaked through his shirt, soaked through the tops of his slacks.

"Gene, Gene!"

"I'm all alright, baby."

"You ain't going to be for long, Castle. Neither's the bitch. I got the notebooks now so I don't need her."

Castle saw him through Bart's shattered window. The gun to her head.

"You think I don't know who you are, Redman? I mean Rosen. Think I don't know you killed Larry Sobell and Cyril Fremont?"

"That show's how much you know, Castle. I didn't kill either of them. You're just a stupid, small-time gumshoe. I told you long ago, you'll always be hunting down grifters stiffed two bit whores like this one here. But you just ran out of always. I'm going to kill you and the bitch. And then the bitch's husband unless somebody else does it first. Now you back away from the car."

"I'm not going anywhere, Rosen."

The man fired, the shot hitting the fender with a blunt sound like a rock wrapped in wool.

"Don't call me that, Castle."

"You like Redman better, eh? Doesn't sound Jewish at all. That's how way you like it, eh? Well maybe so Rosen but you're still a kike."

He fired again, the shot hitting the back window on the driver's side. In his peripheral vision, Castle saw Frontenac walking out.

"Bildorf, that one's touch and go, Rosen. The anti-Semites might raise an eyebrow at that one. The other one's the one I like best. You pick up pocket change shipping your fellow kikes back to Germany, you think serving your Fuhrer's going to change your nasty little secret? What say, Jewboy?"

"Get away from the fucking car, Castle, and when I'm in it, I'll let the dame go. Yeah, then right before I kill her husband I'll let him know she fell for somebody else. But, hey, Doctor Redl, I'll tell him, it's all right cause I shot the bastard."

"You're not going to shoot me, Rosen."

Castle edged to the side, toward the front of the car, his right hand down at his side, tip of the blade in his fingers, knife handle pointing at the street.

"I'm moving toward you, Rosen. And I'm taking the girl. You're not really going to do anything, are you? All you kikes are yellow, everybody knows that."

"Your mistake, Castle."

Rosen raised the gun. Castle kept edging sideways.

"No, it's your mistake!" Frontenac shouting. "Drop it!"

The man spun to face the voice, left arm still locked around the woman's neck, throwing down on Frontenac, exposing his right side to Castle, giving him the time to imagine the blade finding its mark. And then Castle threw.

There was a gasp from the man as the blade went in. It straightened him up, and he spun toward Castle. He went up on his toes like he'd long ago decided he was going to take up ballet if it was the last thing he ever did, and the time had come. He seemed to pirouette, rather gracefully considering his usual hunched movements. He went around another 360 degrees. And he was looking at Castle with genuine astonishment. Castle noting the guy was genuinely ugly. And then he collapsed like Nijinski, a lump of wounded fawn.

Castle looked from the dying man to the woman. Then like a sargeant checking his troops, he glanced over at Frontenac and turned the other way to Raymond Thomas. Castle had the thought, why are Raymond's arms extended in front of him and why is there a gun in his hands?

"Gene!" Castle looked at her and she was pointing, pointing at the gun that was levelled at him from the pavement. Castle was out of ammunition. The ugly man grimaced with pain from the knife in his side but he stopped grimacing when the shot hit him in the leg. It was as if the new wound had cancelled the old one. Castle turned in time to see Raymond Thomas drop the revolver.

The man on the pavement had taken the bullet in the meat of his thigh but still held on to the gun. Castle kicked it out of his hand.

They stood looking down at him.

"You got something to tell me?"

"Yeah, Castle," he gasped. "Fuck you."

"I know where you stashed Redl. What I want to know is who's this guy with the charming handle, Mr. Death."

"Find the kike and you find Mr. Death. You know what Death is in German, don't you Castle? They only got a couple of hours before the boat sails. I'm telling you this because I want you to go after him. You'll never see daybreak, pal."

The ugly man died.

Then she was in his arms. He felt her shudder.

"It's okay now, baby. It's okay."

"I was so scared."

"You were wonderful, Louise."

He held her tightly.

"You know who that is, Louise?" Castle asked her as they looked down at the dead man.

"Yeah, that's Charlie-boy Shantz."

Frontenac had come out from between the cars, and Castle called to him to phone for an ambulance.

They went to Raymond Thomas. He was on his stomach, arms still straight out in front of him.

"Raymond, are you conscious?"

"Yeah, Gene." It came out in a murmur. "But I'm hurt bad. Chest hurts. Legs crushed. Pain is bad."

"Joe made the call. You saved my life, pal."

Raymond smiled. Castle thinking, And I've been suspicious of you.

They stayed with him until Frontenac came back, out of breath. "Ambulance will be here in a couple of minutes."

"Raymond we got to go, Louise and I. We got a date with Mr. Death. You talk to Joe. Stay awake now, til they get here."

"Yeah, Gene. And you stay alive."

"I intend to. Joe, handle the cops, eh? We're on our way."

They went to the Packard, Louise giving Castle a hand, pulling Bart from behind the wheel and dumping his body on the street. Louise climbed in, dress riding up her legs. Castle noticing as he got behind the wheel.

"Fine time to be thinking about that," Louise said.

"Maybe it's all the excitement."

"Couldn't be how I'm dressed, eh? Who I'm impersonating?"

"There's only one for me, doll. And you know who."

She snuggled up to him.

"Help me turn the wheel, I can't use my left arm."

They had six blocks to cover. Castle was able to throw knives and shoot guns but he couldn't drive a Packard all by himself. The night was what was called pitch black, the streets empty and wearing a sheen like they'd been varnished. He thought of the expression about how it was always darkest just before dawn. And everything seemed strangely calm.

Louise said, "How about Little Joe, eh? A regular gunslinger."

"Learned to shoot in Spain. What a guy. Never underestimate him."

They were quiet then until turning down Gore Avenue, Princess Street a block away.

"There's Art Sprague at the side of the building," Castle said. "You can just make him out in the glare from the window."

"Yeah, and what a window it is."

There was a weak blue fluorescent lamp in the display window, giving a glow to a chorus line of artificial legs. Some were legs that went all the way up to where a hip would be, some only so far as non-existent knees; male legs, female legs, made of wood and made of plaster. All in a row. Above them, extending in a half-circle from the leg on the far left to the leg on the far right, were hands and arms and parts of arms. Castle had a vision of the trenches back in '15, hands being blown off, floating up to the sky.

The sign above the window:

Prosthetic Limbs
Good As New

"Now what's real obvious about that window display?" Castle said, looking up from loading his revolver.

"I don't know but it sure is eerie."

"They're all white arms and hands and legs. Or, rather, sort of a pink and tan colour. You're Chinese you can get away with having one of them, I guess. But there aren't any brown ones. What do you do if you're a negro or a fellow from India, and you need new legs? Say, you get runover, legs crushed by a maniac in a car, eh?"

"Guess, you get out your paint set," Louise said. She'd turned the rearview mirror her way, and was applying make-up to her eyelids. "Do it yourself. Or wait until there's a better world and you can get a new limb no matter what colour you are. Sounds like a song that big fellow Paul Robeson should sing."

"Yes, ma'am there's a new day adawning."

"Yeah," Louise said. "In about an hour."

She opened the door, gave him a sultry, come hither glance,

"Do I look like her?"

"Yeah, only better."

"Good, here I go."

"Break a leg, kid."

"How appropriate."

She walked away from the car, diagonally across the intersection of Princess and Gore to the prosthetic limb company, high heels clicking in the rain, neon outlined her curves and made a blue aureole about her head.

Art Sprague came out of the shadows, said something to her, Louise nodded and Art flattened himself at the side of the door as she knocked. Castle watched as they stood waiting, motionless in their positions. He thought of those stark pictures he'd seen by that painter, Hooper or Hopper. Bleak city streets, greasy spoons, nightowls with no place to go. This would make a good picture, a burly rounder and a gorgeous dame, like statues, four-thirty in the morning, by the side door of a place that made artificial limbs.

The picture came to life when, a moment later, someone else was in the doorway. This person was just a vague outline until the door opened wider, and Art Sprague jumped in front of Louise, grabbed the outline that had turned into a man and pulled him outside, knocking him down. Art closed on him, kicked him in the jaw and laid him out. Then Art was on top of the poor fellow, pounding the back of the man's head against the pavement.

It was quick and brutal and effective. Art straightened up and gave the high sign. Castle left the car and made the walk over. He glanced at the man out cold on the pavement and followed Art and Louise inside.

A corridor lead back to a staircase. Doors on the right were for the artificial limb business. They stopped at the stairs. Art, Louise, Castle. No sounds from above. Light coming from an opened door at the bottom. Faint strains of music that grew louder as they descended.

What they saw in that first room were work tables, sinks, molds, tools, artificial arms and legs hanging from the ceiling.The second room was dark and they couldn't make out anything at first. Castle ran his hand along either side of the door looking for a light switch. A voice said, "I will tend to the light."

There were two of them at the far end of the room in front of another door. Four small iron doors were set into the wall to the left. One of the men was pretty big for a guy who wasn't in a sideshow. Bigger than Abel Hibbs. Maybe six foot eight and muscle bound. What with his hair dyed black and combed forward like that, face powdered white, with black eyeliner and pencilled lashes, he was sort of pretty too, if you went for that sort of thing. Or, rather, half his face was pretty. It was as if someone had drawn a line from the middle of his scalp to the dimple in his chin, left one side smooth and sliced up the other side with dozens of little flicks from a knife or a sword. Somebody, or several somebodies, must have held him down and done it to him, and his expression gave you the idea he'd spent every waking moment since taking revenge on whoever was handy. He had a luger in a holster around his left shoulder.

But the other man, in the black double-breasted suit, no more than six foot tall, of medium, even slender build, with only one scar on only one cheek, was somehow scarier. It was the eyes that did it, pale blue ones that saw through you and beyond you.

Looking at the man, Castle knew it was him and not the giant who had taken care of Abel Hibbs.

"So, I suppose you're Mr. Death."

The eyes focused on him. They seemed to flicker from Louise to Castle, like a reptile's.

"My name is Tod. Gustav Tod."

It seemed almost polite, the way he regarded Castle. A thin smile. No contempt in his voice or expression.

"I wonder if you happened to meet Eric, my associate on your way into the building?"

"Eric? Oh, yeah. He must be the fellow who's laying down on the job on the pavement outside."

"And the others?"

"You mean, Bob and Bart and Charlie-boy Shantz, also known as Bildorf, Redman, or Rosen? Of the three, Bob, perhaps, will live."

"So what do you think of that, Mr. Tough guy?"

Art said it. Tod fixed him with killer eyes and looked away, dismissing him.

"We're here for Dr. Redl," Castle said.

"Unfortunately, for you, Dr. Redl, who is in the next room, is leaving on a long journey in just a few minutes."

"The only place he's going is with us," Art Sprague said, but Gustav Tod didn't register that he'd heard anything. He addressed Castle, "So you are the soldier of fortune I've heard about."

"Yeah, that's me."

The guy had only the trace of an accent.

"How'd you know?"

"But I know all about you. I have a good informant. A lady of my aquaintance. Miss Easely."

"Laura? Yeah. You're a real tough character. Knocking her around like that."

"I would never do such a thing. Strike a woman. But Axel would. You see, Miss Easely objected to him borrowing her makeup."

He spoke to the giant in German and the giant laughed, rolled his eyes.

"Please tell me," Tod said. "Why your lady friend Miss Jones is dressed to look like Mrs. Redl?"

"Oh, for chrissakes," Louise muttered.

"But, really, darling." Tod said. "You are quite good. As a matter of fact, let us see how the doctor reacts to your presence. First, of course, Axel will have to search you both."

The giant began with Castle, didn't find the knife. Castle wondering why he always got away with it. Axel looked from Louise to his boss who nodded.

"Axel, here, does not seem to care for this part of it. Having to touch a woman. Indeed, one might call Axel a misogynist of the first order. He served under me in the other war, in Africa and later in the South Seas, and first came to my attention after he disposed of three officers foolish enough to tease him about certain sexual proclivities. I saved him from the firing squad and he has been faithful as a dog to me ever since."

When the giant was done with Louise, he patted down Art Sprague. Castle thinking Art would do something but he didn't. Axel found the automatic in Art's back pocket, stuck it in his waistband and grinned at his boss.

Tod glanced at Axel and nodded, and that's when Art made his move, leaping past the giant to grab the boss from behind. He had fifty pounds on the German but two seconds could not have passed before Art was flat on his back, looking at the ceiling with the German's right shoe across his face. Castle could hardly be sure if he had actually seen Art go over the man's shoulder. Tod's left foot was on the floor but he raised it so all the weight transferred to his right, and Art screamed as the bone in his nose shattered.

Tod spoke again to the giant who stepped forward, bent to grab Art's lapels in his hands and hauled him up. Two hundred and twenty-five pounds, and Axel hoisted him like he was a sack of flour. Axel got him upright, shoved him chest first into a work table, and slammed his right knee into the middle of Art's back. The bartender collapsed onto the floor. He was still groaning when they went into the other room.

Castle's first impulse was to shield his eyes from the light. There were burning candles, it seemed like hundreds of them, on ledges four feet off the floor that ran around the room.

Heinrich Redl was seated in a Morris chair, a book in his lap, a pair of spectacles in his hands. His legs, covered with a Hudson's Bay blanket, were stretched in front of him, heels on a footstool. There were shelves of books behind him. A little table with his medicine on it. There was a larger table a couple of paces from the chair. He could have been a scholar in his basement study except for the bars that kept him at one end of the basement room. Redl must have been dozing because he looked up with a startled expression, put his glasses on. When his eyes focused on the visitors, he got to his feet. Castle thinking, the guy's barely forty but looks twenty years older. An old sixty. And the longing with which he said, "Galatea. Oh, Galatea, *mein liebling*," might have broken your heart if it didn't sound so pathetic, and it only sounded pathetic if you knew the truth.

Tod made laughing sounds but there wasn't any laughter in his eyes.

"You see, my pretty," Tod said. "As I said, you really are quite good. But I'm afraid the merriment has to end. We must go now and board our ship."

Tod spoke to Redl in German and the man obediently backed away from the bars and sat in his chair, never taking his eyes from

Louise.

It was then that Castle noticed the head on the larger table in Redl's cell. He thought, at first, that it was a particularly life-like, if hideous, sculpture. But it was real. A real head on its neck, mounted on a vertical rod set in a block of cedar. The complexion was sallow, sparse brown hair. Castle noting the limp curls. The eyes were brown, the chin receding.

"I see you looking at Dr. Nussbaum," Tod said. "A fine job, yes? And we have Axel to thank. He had much time at his disposal, months, a couple of years, in fact, to devote to learning taxidermy while he was in the Madenhoff hospital. All the typical Jewish ugliness preserved by the taxidermist's art. Unfortunately, Alex won't be able to complete his latest project, one very large Negro hand, recently acquired. Bringing the hand with us on the ship is impractical. It's already beginning to rot."

"So it was your gorilla here who beat Abel Hibbs, tied him to the tree, cut his hands off?"

"My gorilla? You mean my gorilla against your ape? It started out that way, but..." Tod raised one eyebrow, glanced rather sadly it seemed, at Axel. "But the ape struck first and that single blow of his paw put paid to my gorilla. So it was left to me to subdue the ape and bind him to the tree."

Castle stared at him, believing him but not being able to figure it. "I hope he at least hurt you a little."

"Do I appear hurt? When Axel regained consciousness, I permitted him to saw off the ape's hands."

Doctor Redl was still sitting there looking at Louise with almost palpable longing. Near him on the table, Dr. Nussbaum wasn't looking at anything.

"What about Nussbaum?" Castle asked.

"He was not as important as our Herr Doctor Redl; hence, there was no need to send him back to the Fatherland. So. The rest of him, you are curious about. Perhaps you noticed the ovens in the other room? That is where they bake the plaster arms and legs and the ovens serve other purposes as well. But our Dr. Redl will not meet the same fate as Nussbaum."

"You're right, he won't," Castle said. "He's coming with us."

Tod didn't even look angry at this. Castle had realized right away that fear and Mr. Tod were not acquainted but, now, Castle was down to hoping for, at least, a trace of mild annoyance. What he got instead was an expression of genuine curiosity.

"How on earth do you propose to bring that about?" Tod said, and switched to German to give an order to Axel. The giant had just nodded, and made the first step toward Castle when they heard the noise on the stairs.

"Hell's everybody?" a loud voice called. "Goddamn ain't fair, I got—whoops!—fella could take a tumble on these damn steps. Ain't right I got to drink alone."

They heard someone bump into a wall and take the lord's name in vain.

"Lot's of hands around here. Holy Jesus. How'd do? How'd do? Sorry fellows I can't shake hands with all of you."

Tod spoke to Axel who went into the other room and came back holding a staggering Frank Evans by the scruff of the neck. He stank of booze but kept a firm grip on a quart bottle, a quarter full of rye whiskey. "Have a drink, big fella, warm you up. Must get mighty cold up there where you are."

"You disappoint me, Frank," Castle said. "I was counting on you."

"Sorry, old buddy. I guess I, I don't know, I kind of got lonesome out there. Waiting all that time in the dark. Thought a little sip wouldn't hurt. You want one?"

"No, I don't, Frank."

"Hell I don't want to drink alone. How about you?" he said to Tod, who looked back at Frank like he was a harmless bug.

"Oh, there's a fellow in jail. Hey, buddy?" Frank went over, gripped the bars and looked at Redl. "Here, buddy. I know what it's like. Have a wee taste. Let me tell you about the time the bulls threw me in the joint in Fort William. Just dropped off a sidedoor Pullman, see..."

But, Frank, instead of spinning his yarn, began to sing, swinging the bottle to keep time. "All around the water tower waiting for a train..."

Tod spoke again to Axel, this time biting off his order. The giant was three feet away when Frank broke the bottle across his head. And on the back swing, he slashed the good side of Axel's face. Dazed, with blood in his eyes, Axel blindly grabbed for Frank, and Frank brought his knee up between the man's legs. Brought it up again and another time. Still, Axel managed to get Frank in a bear hug. As Castle moved forward to help, he had a picture in his peripheral vision of Gustav Tod watching imperturbably. He stopped then and took the knife from the sheath at his ankle.

Before Castle got two steps closer, Louise pulled off one of her shoes, grasped it by the toe, and brought the heel down on the crouching giant's skull. Castle thinking, the guy's head is so hard it's only going in an inch or so. But it put him down and stuck. The big man lying there with his legs curled up, hands between them, face a mask of blood, the point of the shoe's heel stuck in his head. Frank beside him grasping for air. Both of them in broken glass.

"That was good," Gustav Tod said. "I was fooled by the charade. But now it is time for me to leave with the jew, Redl. Please stand aside. I will kill you and the woman or not kill you, it is all the same to me."

"We're not standing aside."

"Don't be foolish. How can you stop me?"

Castle had the knife out from under his coat cuff.

"Like this," he said and threw.

The four inch blade entered the right side of Gustav Tod's chest less than a hands' width below his collarbone.

The German flinched and backed away half a step but in a moment had regained his composure.

"That's pretty good, Mr. Death. Stick a knife in you and you stay cool. How do you do that?"

"It is discipline and will power. Now what is your next trick?"

"Tell you the truth, Gustav. I'm fresh out of ideas. I guess I'll have to come over and try to beat you up."

"By all means, yes. Please come and try."

It was then that Frank slid the gun across the floor, the one that Axel had taken from Art Sprague.

"Hey," said Castle, grabbing it. "Here's an idea."

And he fired, the bullet striking Tod on the other side of his chest, just above the heart. Tod fell back against the bars of Redl's cell. Castle assumed the man would slide to the floor and he started to but in a moment he'd regained his excellent posture, or most of it.

"See the thing is, Mr. Death." Still no expression on Tod's face. No hatred, anger, fear, nothing decipherable. "Your weakness is, you think you're invincible."

Tod turned his head to speak to Redl. The Doctor rose from his armchair and when he was at the bars, Tod reached and took him by the neck. One hand on either side of a bar. Tod squeezed. Castle shot him in the right side. Tod relaxed his grip but it was the doctor who fell gasping to the floor.

Finally, Tod, taking a couple of steps, appeared a little unsteady. He walked like a fellow who'd had a few more than a few but was upright and determined to walk all the way home. He made his way to the luggage and grabbed the handle of a big suitcase of Moroccan leather. Castle marvelling that he could lift the thing.

"I must be going now," Tod said, and walked out of the room.

"Yeah. Auf wiedersehen, pal."

They heard him taking the first couple of stairs.

"Jesus Christ," Louise muttered. "How can he do that?"

"I wonder what odds Beanie Brown would give, him making it to the street."

They heard more footsteps but no sound of a body falling.

Louise and Castle climbed the stairs.

It was dawn. They were surprised to see a weak sun peeking over the still wet street way down at the east end of Princess. Surprised to see Gustav Tod staggering toward it. He let go of the suitcase.

"The man's headed east to the Fatherland," Castle said. "Guess he figures he can buy new duds when he gets there."

Tod nearly made it across Gore Avenue before collapsing on his back.

They stared at him for a few seconds before Louise said, "Well I guess that did it."

"Yeah."

They walked into the intersection where Tod lay motionless. Blood spread like ink blots around the two bullet holes but oozed from the wound the knife had made below his shoulder. His blue eyes were open, same colour as the morning sky.

"Now that was one tough son-of-a-bitch," Castle said. They both bent over to get a closer look, as if there was something in death that would reveal the man's secret.

Castle looked into the guy's blue eyes, and the corpse's head lifted.

Louise screamed.

Tod's right hand, the one that concealed the knife that he'd pulled from his chest, swung up and the blade left a trail across Castle's cheek.

Castle stumbled backwards and landed on his rear end. One hand went to his face. He looked at Tod.

Mr. Death smiled at him as he lowered his head. The smile still on his face as he finally died.

They heard the sirens.

"Here comes Koronicki," Louise said.

The Chief of Detectives didn't like what he was seeing as he disembarked from his unmarked and barked orders at his men. He headed for the basement of the prosthetic limb company and nothing down there improved his humour.

"Jesus Christ, Castle." he said, a few minutes later. "I know I owe you—make that owed you, but I've been paying you back like crazy these last few days."

"Yes, Detective."

"You're messy. Very messy. Leave a trail of dead and maimed wherever you go. In the old days, everything would be cleaner. Mr. Larry Sobell, a charred corpse. Cyril Fremont with two slugs in him. Both of them invoking—is that the right word?"

"I don't know yet."

"Invoking your name. You didn't know I know about Fremont, eh? Then there's two dead guys over on Homer Street. Well good riddance to them bums, especially the creep called Charlie-boy Shantz who is long overdue. But your own pal, the shine, lying there in the middle of the street, he couldn't move. Only could groan. We catch the flash from your hotshot reporter pal and we get there just as some good citizen's coming down the street; the good citizen see's a bloody mess of a white man over here, a groaning negro individual over there, not to mention the dead caucasian on the pavement, and what does he do, the good citizen? He veers to the left when he sees the shine, veers to the right when he sees the caucasian and keeps on going, like it's a driver's test. Four o'clock in the morning, guy's been out having some drinks. He's gonna wake up later, see in his mind the picture of all that, tell himself, no it couldn't have happened. Maybe he'll vow to give up the booze, eh? So they'll be one less drunk bozo driving home."

"May I interrupt to inquire about Raymond?"

"You just did. Interrupt that is. He's, uh, I wouldn't say he's all right but he'll live. Report I get is that he'll even walk again. Maybe before this new war's over if it lasts awhile. Fellow who ought to be put away though is your reporter buddy, going around playing the hero."

"Well, he was."

"Yeah, I bet. And now I get here and what do I see?. I see this dead man in the middle of Princess and Gore. You, one cheek just sliced open, still got the stitches in the other one. Downstairs some monster with woman's make-up and about a million scars. The make-up in the cuts puts me in mind of scum between the logs in the saltchuck. Oh, yeah and then there's the high heel shoe sticking out of his head. Which reminds me of another case, a week and a half, two weeks ago. Art Sprague—who's going to have an aching back for a long time—I see him in a room full of fake arms and legs. I see Frank Evans, that anarcho-syndacalist hobo, lying there drunk as usual. There's another guy hardly speaks a word of English in a god-damned cell. About a million candles all around. And, oh, yeah, then there's the perfectly preserved human head on a table in the cell. And the ovens. Bones in one of them. A negro hand in another. Jesus Christ, Castle why don't you get some nice clean kind of operative work like guys sneaking around on their wives or vicey versey?"

"Now, look Horace.."

"Shhh! for Chrissakes." Koronicki looked around anxiously. "I told you not to call me that in public."

Three cops were approaching, two uniforms and a guy in a suit.

"Murphy! Olafson!" shouted Koronicki. "Citizens have started to appear."

The guy in the suit kept coming. Koronicki jerked a thumb at him.

"Castle, Miss Jones. This is Danny Bartoli. My new partner."

Castle didn't even have time to think: Oh, no. Not another one to deal with—because the young detective smiled and stuck out his hand.

"Hey, I'm glad to meet you. And you, ma'am. I've heard a lot about you two."

They shook hands, Castle saying, "Your boss been shooting off his mouth, eh?"

"Yeah. No. I mean, I even heard about you before that. Few years ago."

"Yeah, tell me a little of it then I got to get out of here on account of I might bleed to death."

"Yeah, it was you caused my uncle to get busted, sent back to Calabria."

"Hey, I'm sorry. Detective."

"It's all right. He was the black sheep of the family, worked for that gangster Garmano."

"Your uncle wouldn't be a big galoot, called Marco?"

"No way, not that bum. Vince is my uncle. Guy with the hook nose."

Detective Bartoli turned and gave them his profile, grinning bashfully. "Runs in the family. You remember my uncle?

"Oh, yes, indeed I do," Castle said.

"It's an elegant nose, Detective," Louise said.

"Hey, thank you, ma'am."

"Finally," Castle said.

"Finally, what?" Koronicki said.

"You got a partner that's a human being."

"Yeah, and you can get better acquainted as he drives you to St. Paul's for your daily stitches."

They walked over to a cruiser, Detective Bartoli saying, "So tell me about Uncle Vince."

"Well, what I remember most is the guy always needed a shave," Castle said as they got in the car. "Face was the colour of Ovaltine. Ovaltine with ants in it. That and the fact he tried to kill me on two or three occasions..."

CHAPTER FIFTEEN

It was three weeks later, eight o'clock in the morning at Ramona's Cafe, and they were celebrating Raymond Thomas' first morning out of the hospital. Guy Roberts had brought him around in a special wheelchair. Both Raymond's legs were in casts, and sticking straight out in front of him on the leg rests. There was another guy in a wheelchair too, Danny Klein. Raymond had lost fifteen pounds but he was in good spirits, considering; he smiled, sipped of the rum-laced coffee. It was a rare occurrence, Roberts sitting anywhere in Ramona's except at the counter. The sugar king saying little, attentive to his pal.

Louise and Castle were in the booth across from Art Sprague and Laura Easely. Frontenac and Frank Evans had dragged chairs up to the booth. It was the first time they'd all been together to tell war stories.

"You should have seen Frank take on that giant." Castle said to Danny and Laura. Then looking at Frank: "You were after him like a wildcat, partner."

Frank nodded, "Not bad for an ex-vacuum cleaner salesman."

"And then there's Dead Eye Frontenac."

The reporter beamed and shrugged. "All the pistol practice over in Spain came in handy."

Then he tried to look serious, saying, "But, of course, one never knows how one will act in times of crisis."

"You're right, Joe. One don't."

"I was just fortunate," the reporter said, solemnly, "that the gods chose me to be a hero."

They laughed at that, and after a moment, Frontenac laughed too.

Laura poured rum all around, raised her own glass, "I'd like to propose a toast to Gene who, never having approved of any of my boyfriends, finally killed one of them."

After they'd drank to that, Art Sprague touched a tender finger to his swollen nose, said, "I wouldn't have minded if those gods had of chosen me."

"They did, Art. The way you got us into the building, what'd you mean?"

"I mean, the other thing."

"Hell, man. There were two of them."

"I'm lying on the floor, looking up at them fake arms and legs. I couldn't move because of my back and I'm thinking I'm never going to walk again."

"But you're getting around okay, now."

"Sure, Gene but I got to wear this harness, like a goddamned girdle."

Laura patted his forearm, saw that Castle had noticed the gesture, and stuck her tongue out at him.

"Speaking of girdles," Louise said. "I had to squeeze into one to try and pass as that slinky dame. And if that wasn't bad enough, since we had to cut my hair and do a fast dye job, whole time we're out on the street—it's all misty—and I'm worrying not so much about getting hurt as about it starting to rain again and the dye running."

"Vanity, vanity," Raymond intoned in his best rumbling baritone.

"So sayeth you," Louise remarked, and pointed her glass to him.

"Funny thing is," Castle said. "You fooled the husband but not the Nazi."

The door of Ramona's opened.

And there was Galatea Monti.

She took a few steps inside, followed by Heinrich Redl, her husband who might have been her father. It grew quiet as, one by one, people turned to look.

She had on a green dress, a fox stole over her shoulders, heels and silk stockings.

Castle noticed Frontenac staring at her with his open mouth. Even Matty Muldoon over there looked transfixed, tea mug suspended halfway between the counter and his open mouth. There was some guy next to Matty, a guy who looked like a Guatemalan or a gypsy or basque fisherman, who made himself conspicuous, to Castle, at least, because he merely glanced at the woman and turned his attention back to his mug of coffee.

"This, obviously, must be the helmet-headed one herself," Laura muttered.

"What I wouldn't give to be able to make an entrance like that," Louise said.

She came walking toward the table or, rather, gliding toward it. The husband behind her.

Castle had spoken with them twice in the last three weeks. They both had profusely expressed their gratitude. Or, at least, Redl had expressed himself profusely. He was a good man, Castle knew that. He did important work. He was valuable to the war effort. Anybody's war effort. But, still.

They were bound for the States, for California, for Los Angeles. Redl was going to work for the American government. She was going to sing at Ivy Anderson's place in South Central.

"We have taxi waiting," Redl said, with his heavy accent. "We take now train to California."

Castle was the first to stand up and shake his hand.

"We may never see you again but we will always be remembering you." Redl spoke, looking at Castle, then at the others. "You will be in my dreams. Goodbye."

Castle noting that his look had encompassed everyone, including Guy, Danny and Laura.

Galatea Monti looked at them too but she reversed the order, Castle last, her gaze holding on to him for a beat, "Yes, you will be in my dreams, also."

She turned quickly away and went to the door.

In that beat, Castle had seen her eyes start to mist. He hoped no one else had.

In a minute the woman and her husband were gone, through the door, into a taxi and out of their lives.

They stared after her. Not them, it was her that they stared after.

Matty Muldoon broke the silence, calling to Castle across the restaurant, his voice like a foghorn, "Jesus, lad. Who was the traffic stopper?"

"That, Matty?" Castle said, "That was just some dame who likes to mingle.

CHAPTER SIXTEEN

An hour later, Castle and Louise, Frontenac and Danny Klein were still in the booth at Ramona's, and working on a second bottle of rum. The rest of the regulars had gone away and at least a dozen individuals had come and gone playing musical stools up at the counter but the man with the moustache who could have been a Guatemalan or a gypsy or basque fisherman was still there. Maude was in the back taking her break so Louise slid out of the booth to get a pot of coffee from Sammy Wong, in case anyone still cared to camoflage or ruin their rum. Danny Klein hadn't cared to since his initial drink and now, having reached his sixth or seventh, was saying to Castle: "Ever since we talked about it in Manny Israel's backroom, I've been trying to remember the words. You know the one's I mean."

"Sure. Danny. And did you remember them?"

"I got some of them. Let's see. 'When the years pass by and the wounds of war are...'"

"'Are staunched.'" Castle prompted him.

"Yeah, and, uh, 'when the cloudy memory of sorrowful, bloody days returns in a present of freedom, love and well-being....'oh, hell."

"'Speak to your children. Tell them of the International Brigades,'" Louise came to the table with the coffee pot. "Tell them how, coming over the seas and mountains, crossing frontiers bristling with bayonets, these men reached our country as crusaders for freedom. They gave up everything....'"

Louise looked at Danny, continued, "'their loves, their country, home and fortune....Today they are going away. Many of them, thousands of them, are staying here with the Spanish earth for their shroud.'"

"That was all to the women," Castle said. "Then she addressed the men. She said..."

"'You can go proudly.'"

They, all four, looked up toward the new voice. It was the guy with the moustache. He had spun around on his stool to face them.

"'You are history. You are legend. You are the heroic example of democracy's solidarity and universality.'"

His accent was as hard to account for as his face.

"'We shall not forget you. And, when the olive tree of peace puts forth its leaves again, come back!'"

"That's very good, partner," Danny Klein said. "Were you over there?"

"Yes, sir," the man answered, looked from Danny to Castle. "I was indeed"

"You want to join us, have a drink?" Danny asked him.

The man said he should be be going but supposed he could linger long enough for a drink.

When the man slid off the stool, Castle noticed his black shoes wore a mirror shine and there was nary a wrinkle in all of his grey garbadine suit. He was about five eleven, black hair parted in the middle, his black moustache had a part too. Cops didn't dress like that, Castle thought.

The guy stood over the table and Danny poured him a couple of fingers of rum. The man raised his glass. "'Long live our comrades, the heroes of the International Brigades.'"

"Yeah," Danny nodded. "That was the last thing she said. *La Pasionaria.*"

"Okay, so what do we do now," Castle said. "Sing the Internationale?"

"Why the bloody hell not?" Danny said.

"Before we do that," Castle said. "I want to make sure I know the names of everybody in the choir."

After the man said his name the rest of them, except for Castle, introduced themselves. Then they looked at him, wondering why he hadn't said anything.

"Where're your manners, boy?" Danny said, slurring his words. "Looks like we got a comrade here."

"It is not necessary," the man said. "I know very well who he is. We have mutual friends, one very special one in particular. But I wonder, Gene Castle, if you know who I am?"

"Yes, Leandro Martine. I do, indeed, know who you are."

"What racket you in, Mr. Martine?" Joe Frontenac asked, looking at the man curiously.

"Why, Joe," Castle answered for the man. "Mr. Martine, also known as Senor, Monsieur, Herr, Citizen, Field Marshall, or Commandante, and you can pick from a score or so of other surnames, is a man of many, well, rackets may not be the proper word, let's just say he has shown up in more places under more guises than the goddamned Comte de Saint Germaine."

Martine nodded formally at Castle, "But let us say, though I may be equally damned, I have, at least, shown up on the opposite side to that of the infamous Comte."

"That is true," Castle said, and two men smiled at each other.

"I'll take my leave now," Martine nodded. "We must talk soon," he said to Castle.

When he was gone, Louise said, "That's the guy you'd figure to be Galatea Monti's husband."

"So who the hell is he?" Frontenac wanted to know. "What is he? I sense a story."

"You reporters are always misusing a word that if it fits anybody fits that guy."

"Come on, what the hell word is that?'

"Legend."

"Oh, yeah? And what does this legend's appearance in our fair city portend, for chrissakes?"

"For me," Castle said, "It probably portends a whole heap of trouble."

AGMV Marquis

Member of the Scabrini Group

Quebec, Canada
2000